PRAISE FOR

DONNA GRANT'S
**New York Times best-selling
romance novels**

DARK KINGS SERIES

"A breathtaking tale...I absolutely loved it!"
–Romance Junkies on Dark Craving

"The author has created a fantastic and mesmerizing fantasy world with intriguing twists, surprises and unique elements that keeps the reader turning the pages to the very end."
–Night Owl Reviews on Dark Heat

DARK WARRIORS SERIES

"Evie and Malcolm is a couple that makes it impossible not to love them."
–The Jeep Diva

"Grant's smoldering seventh Dark Warrior outing will grip readers from the first page, immersing them in her wounded, lonely couple's journey of redemption...each scene is filled with Grant's clever, complex characters and trademark sizzle."
–Romantic Times Magazine (RT Book Reviews)

D0839046

Don't miss these other spellbinding novels by
DONNA GRANT

ROGUES OF SCOTLAND SERIES

The Craving
The Hunger
The Tempted

CHIASSON SERIES

Wild Fever
Wild Dream
Wild Need

DARK KING SERIES

Dark Heat
Darkest Flame
Fire Rising
Burning Desire
Hot Blooded

DARK WARRIOR SERIES

Midnight's Master
Midnight's Lover
Midnight's Seduction
Midnight's Warrior
Midnight's Kiss
Midnight's Captive
Midnight's Temptation
Midnight's Promise
Midnight's Surrender

DARK SWORD SERIES

Dangerous Highlander
Forbidden Highlander
Wicked Highlander
Untamed Highlander
Shadow Highlander
Darkest Highlander

SHIELD SERIES

A Dark Guardian
A Kind of Magic
A Dark Seduction
A Forbidden Temptation
A Warrior's Heart

DRUIDS GLEN SERIES

Highland Mist
Highland Nights
Highland Dawn
Highland Fires
Highland Magic
Dragonfyre

SISTERS OF MAGIC TRILOGY

Shadow Magic
Echoes of Magic
Dangerous Magic

Royal Chronicles Novella Series

Prince of Desire
Prince of Seduction
Prince of Love
Prince of Passion

Wicked Treasures Novella Series

Seized by Passion
Enticed by Ecstasy
Captured by Desire

Stand Alone Stories

Savage Moon (ebook novella)
Forever Mine (ebook novella)
Mutual Desire

And look for more anticipated novels from Donna Grant

The Seduced (Rogues of Scotland)
Night's Blaze (Dark Kings)
Moon Thrall (LaRue)

coming soon!

THE
TEMPTED

ROGUES OF SCOTLAND

DONNA GRANT

THE TEMPTED

© 2014 by DL Grant, LLC
Excerpt from *The Seduced* copyright © 2014 by Donna
Grant

Cover design © 2014 by Leah Suttle

ISBN 10: 1942017103
ISBN 13: 978-1942017103

Available in ebook and print editions

www.DonnaGrant.com

ACKNOWLEDGEMENTS

A special thanks goes out to my wonderful team that helps me get these books out. Hats off to my editor, Chelle Olsen, and cover design extraordinaire, Leah Suttle. Thank you both for helping me to keep my crazy schedule and keeping me sane!

There's no way I could do any of this without my amazing family – Steve, Gillian, and Connor – thanks for putting up with my hectic schedule and for knowing when it was time that I got out of the house. And special nod to the Grant pets – all five – who have no problem laying on the keyboard to let me know it's time for a break.

Last but not least, my readers. You have my eternal gratitude for the amazing support you show me and my books. Y'all rock my world. Stay tuned at the end of this story for a sneak peek of *The Seduced*, Rogues of Scotland book 4 out February 9, 2015. Enjoy!

xoxo
Donna

PROLOGUE

Highlands of Scotland
Summer, 1427

There were only a handful of things in Stefan Kennedy's life that he was thankful for. His three friends – Ronan, Daman, and Morcant – made up the majority of them.

If it weren't for his friends, Stefan knew he would already be dead. The anger inside him was a living beast. He couldn't control it, and he stopped trying long ago. No one had given him a reason to try and keep it in check until he met Morcant, Ronan, and Daman that fateful day.

It was by happenchance that he even went to the Highland Games. He almost hadn't, and he still didn't know what had made him go. But he had. Everything changed upon meeting his friends. Only with them did he have reason to restrain his rage.

His horse snorted, shaking his great head. Stefan patted his steed's neck as he waited with Morcant and Daman for Ronan to arrive. The valley between the two mountains was wide. The summer sun was warm, and a breeze ruffled his horse's white mane.

Above them, the shrill cry of a golden eagle broke the silence. Stefan glanced up at the bird to see it soaring upon the wind currents before flapping its great wings.

Stefan's attention was snapped to the right at the sound of a horse's whinny. He spotted the rider atop the mountain. Finally. Stefan's patience had been wearing thin. Morcant's smile when he saw Ronan had Stefan glancing at Daman, who was also grinning.

Ronan's horse pawed the ground, and a moment later, he leaned forward on his mount. His horse raced down the mountain. Morcant and Daman laughed while Stefan shook his head at Ronan's wildness. Then again, that same thread ran through all four of them. It was just one of many reasons they'd become friends.

Morcant had to hold his young stallion with a firm hand as the three waited for Ronan to reach them. Daman's mount danced sideways, just as Morcant finally got control of his horse and Ronan arrived.

"About time," Stefan grumbled to Ronan.

Ronan raised his brow. "You might want to rein in that temper, my friend. We're going to be around beautiful women this night. Women require smiles and sweet words. No' furrowed brows."

Stefan was used to such words, so Daman and Morcant's laughter didn't bother him. Stefan shot Ronan a humorless look.

"Aye, we've heard enough about this Ana," Daman said as he turned his mount alongside Ronan's. "Take me to this gypsy beauty so I can see her for myself."

Ronan's lips compressed. "You think to take her from me?"

Daman's confident smile grew as his eyes twinkled in merriment. "Is she that beautiful?"

"Just you try," Ronan dared, only half jesting.

"Be cautious, Ronan. You wrong a gypsy, and they'll curse you. No' sure we should be meddling with such people," Morcant said as he shoved his hair out of his eyes.

Morcant wasn't generally the voice of reason among the four. That was normally reserved for Daman, but Morcant's comment gave Stefan pause. Most clans didn't allow gypsies on their land for long. Even though their bold colors and beauty were intriguing, there was no doubt they could be dangerous.

Ronan laughed at Morcant and reined in his jittery mount. "Ah, but with such a willing body, how am I to refuse Ana? Come, my friends. Let us enjoy the bounty that awaits." He gave a short whistle and his horse surged forward in a run again.

Stefan's well-trained mount stood still, his ears pricked forward as Stefan watched Ronan. The three remained behind for a moment as Ronan took the lead as he always did. Each had found their place within their small group. What began by chance a decade earlier had grown into their own clan. After they'd met at the Highland Games, they'd made sure to meet up regularly until they were as inseparable as brothers. The four formed a friendship that grew tighter with each year that passed.

"I'm no' missing this," Morcant said and gave his stallion his head. The horse immediately took off.

Stefan shared a look with Daman, and as one, they nudged their mounts forward. It wasn't long before they caught up with Morcant. Ronan looked over his shoulder, a wide smile on his face. He spurred his mount faster. Morcant then leaned low over his stallion's neck until he pulled up alongside Ronan.

Stefan loosened the reins, and his horse closed the last bit of distance to come even with Ronan a moment before Daman rode up beside Morcant.

A few moments later, Ronan tugged the reins, easing his stallion into a canter so they rode their horses four abreast. Being with his friends and riding along the craggy, windswept mountains were the only things that could make Stefan forget who he was.

His soul felt almost...free.

How he cherished his time with his friends. Without them...well, he didn't want to go down that road. Not now. Not when he was in such a fine mood.

The four rode from one glen to another until Ronan finally slowed his horse to a walk. They stopped atop the next hill and looked down at the circle of gypsy wagons hidden in the wooded vale below.

Stefan focused his gaze on the circle of wagons and the gypsies walking around. There was a large fire in the middle of the camp, and as far as Stefan could tell, no one else was with the gypsies.

"I've a bad feeling," Daman said as he shifted uncomfortably atop his mount. "We shouldna be here."

Morcant's horse flung up his head, and he brought his mount under control with soft words. "I've a need to sink my rod betwixt willing thighs. If you doona wish to partake, Daman, then doona, but you willna be stopping me."

"Nor me," Ronan said.

Stefan was silent for several moments. Never before had he abandoned his friends, and he wasn't about to start now. Unlike Morcant, who wanted to fuck every woman he came across, Stefan tended to only sate his body when he could no longer stand the need.

He would go into the camp with the others, even if only to watch their backs. Stefan gave Ronan a nod of agreement.

Ronan was the first to ride down the hill to the camp, and Morcant was right on his heels. Stefan nudged his horse into a gallop as a young beauty with long black hair came running out to greet

Ronan in her brightly colored skirts. Ronan pulled his horse to a halt and jumped off with a smile as the woman launched herself into his arms. Ronan caught her and brought his lips down to hers.

Stefan pulled his horse to a halt beside Morcant's, and a moment later, Daman rode up on Morcant's other side. By the look of Daman's tightly held lips, he wasn't happy.

Ronan and the woman spoke quietly before Ronan turned her toward them. "Ana, these are my friends, Daman, Morcant, and Stefan," he said, pointing to each of them in turn.

Her smile was wide as she held out her arm to the camp. "Welcome to our camp."

Morcant quickly dismounted and dropped the reins to allow his horse to graze freely. He then started to walk between two wagons towards the center of the camp before he hesitated.

Stefan wasn't going to sit atop his mount as he waited for Ronan and Morcant to sate themselves. He dismounted and patted his horse.

"I'll be back," he mumbled and followed Morcant into the camp. He met Morcant's gaze when Morcant glanced his way. It was Morcant's pause that had Stefan looking back at Daman. Indecision warred on Daman's face.

Stefan didn't move as he waited for Daman to make up his mind. Finally, Daman slid from his horse and gathered the reins of all four mounts to tether them together.

"I'll keep watch," Daman said as he sat outside the camp near a tree.

Ronan wrapped an arm around Ana and walked away calling, "Your loss."

Morcant gave a nod and continued on to a woman sitting on the steps to her wagon, her bright turquoise and yellow skirts dipping between her legs while she braided a leather halter for a horse.

It was long moments before Stefan reached the fire in the middle of the camp and nodded to the three men sitting there.

"Welcome," the youngest of them said. He had black hair and eyes, and wore a bright red shirt and black pants.

The elder of the other two had stark white hair cut short. He was carving a piece of wood into a buck and motioned to the rock next to him. "Have a seat."

Stefan glanced at the third man, middle-aged, with just a hint of white in his dark hair at the temples. His dark eyes were welcoming as he stood and spooned some soup into a bowl then handed it to Stefan.

"Thank you," Stefan said and sat. He sampled a bit of the soup and nodded at the rich flavor. "It's good."

"Of course it is," the youngest said with a laugh. "Our food is excellent."

The elder lifted his eyes to Stefan, his bushy white brows raised on his forehead. "You're friends with Ronan?"

"I am."

"Close friends?"

Stefan paused in his eating. "I consider him a brother, as I do Morcant and Daman."

"When does Ronan plan on marrying Ana then?"

Stefan swallowed. Marry? Apparently, they didn't know Ronan at all. Ronan was as opposed to marriage as the Devil was to Heaven. It wasn't like Stefan could tell them any of that, but surely Ana knew.

Ronan wasn't the type to take a woman to his bed unless she knew from the beginning there would never be more from him. Ronan wasn't cruel, but he also didn't lead a female on.

"He's no' mentioned it to me," Stefan finally said.

The youngest chuckled. "If Ana has her way, it'll be tonight."

"He's all she can talk about," the middle-aged man said. "By the way, we've not introduced ourselves. I'm Yanko. This is my son Luca, and my father Guaril."

Stefan nodded his head to each of them. "I'm Stefan Kennedy."

~ ~ ~

Despite talk of Ronan's impending marriage that he knew nothing about, Stefan finished his meal listening to the three men chatter of their travels. He didn't understand their need to move from place to place. It was almost as if they couldn't remain still. It was partly due to the fact that no one would allow them to remain, but it was also in their blood to wander.

When Guaril finished his carving, he handed it to Stefan to inspect. Stefan was impressed with the skill displayed. Guaril had perfectly captured the likeness of a red deer from the hooves to the eyes to the antlers.

"This is fine craftsmanship, Guaril."

Luca smiled. "My grandfather is a master. We sell many of his carvings."

"I keep trying to teach Luca as I did Yanko," Guaril said with a grin directed at his grandson. "But he lacks the dedication."

Yanko slapped his son on the back. "I was the same. He'll grasp it soon enough."

"Here," Guaril said and tossed the small dagger to Luca.

Surprised, Luca caught it and then held it up over his head causing even Stefan to smile as the three laughed.

The night was suddenly shattered by an anguished scream, a soul-deep, fathomless cry that was dredged from the depths of someone's soul.

Stefan was immediately on guard. He searched the camp and saw Ronan first. He stood outside of Ana's wagon, shirtless with his hand on the hilt of his sword, looking at an old woman who was staring at something in the grass.

The next instant, Morcant hurriedly exited a wagon still fastening his kilt. Stefan slowly stood and glanced behind him to find Daman standing outside the circle of wagons with a resigned expression.

"Who is that?" Luca asked in a strangled whisper.

Stefan turned his gaze back to Ronan and the old woman. That's when he saw the bright pink and blue skirts of the body in the grass. It was Ana, a dagger still sticking out of her stomach. Their night of fun and revelry was over.

By the looks exchanged amongst the gypsies, there was no way Stefan and his friends were going to be able to leave without a fight. The smiles from the gypsies turned to glares of hatred and disgust.

Stefan noticed Morcant's gaze. He gave Morcant a nod to say he was ready for battle because that's exactly what was about to happen.

The gypsies in the camp stood still, almost afraid to move. Ronan's face was twisted with denial and sorrow while Morcant slowly began to pull his sword from his scabbard.

"Ronan," Stefan said urgently, trying to snap his friend to attention. It was going to take all of them to get out alive. Stefan palmed the hilt of his sword and waited.

There was a moment of utter silence, as if the world were holding its breath. Then the old woman let loose a shriek and pointed her gnarled finger at Ronan. Ronan's eyes widened in confusion and anger.

"Ilinca will make him pay," Luca whispered.

Yanko cut his gaze to his son and said, "Enough."

But Stefan didn't need to hear more. He looked

at the old woman again. Her grief shone plainly, clearly. So did her anger.

Words, hurried and unfamiliar, fell from Ilinca's lips. The language was Romany, and Stefan didn't need to understand them to know that nothing good could come from whatever she was saying.

The longer Stefan stared, the more he realized Ronan was being held against his will. His pale green eyes were wide with confusion. The same time Stefan drew his sword, Morcant rushed Ilinca.

The next thing Stefan saw was Ilinca shifting her gaze to Morcant. Instantly, he was frozen in place, no more able to move than Ronan. With Morcant taken care of, Ilinca returned her gaze to Ronan and continued speaking in the strange language.

Stefan couldn't believe that Morcant and Ronan had been halted with merely a look from the old woman. He let loose his rage, let it fill him until he shook with it. He released a battle cry and leapt over the fire toward Ilinca. Stefan hadn't gotten two steps before the old gypsy pinned him with a look that instantly jerked him to a halt.

Stefan was momentarily flabbergasted at the feeling rushing over him, the force controlling his body. He tried to move his arm, his head, anything. But she had complete control. He couldn't even get his lips or voice to work.

The only thing he could move was his eyes, and he wished to God he wasn't able to see what was going on. He hated the helplessness, the utter powerlessness he felt. When he got free – and, he would get free – he was going to take Ilinca's head.

Ronan had no more killed Ana than he had. Ilinca had no right to blame any of them for Ana's weakness. The longer the old gypsy held Stefan in place, the more his fury grew, consuming him with a blind rage that blocked out everything but the gypsy.

Ilinca's gaze held his for a moment, seemingly undeterred by his wrath. She looked behind him.

Daman.

Stefan tried to shout for Daman to get away before she got him, as well. Stefan knew Daman wouldn't leave, and when a satisfied smile crossed the old gypsy's face, Stefan knew Daman had walked into the camp.

Stefan didn't have time to think about that as Ronan suddenly squeezed his eyes shut while his body shook with pain. In the next instant, he vanished.

Naaaayyyyyy!

The bellow welled up in Stefan's mind but it never passed his lips. No sooner had the old woman looked at Morcant than he disappeared, as well.

Then Ilinca returned her gaze to Stefan.

I'm going to kill you!

She smiled coldly, as if she could read his mind. The pain started slowly but built quickly. It seeped into every nerve, every crevice of his body.

It burned, it bit. It slashed, it gutted.

It ravaged.

Stefan held Ilinca's gaze, daring her to give him

all that she had. Had he not been held up by her magic, Stefan would've been on his knees, doubled over from the piercing, searing pain that went on and on.

His vision began to fade until there was nothing but blackness. Stefan fought against Ilinca's hold, against his vision loss and his inability to help his friends.

The pain grew to such a degree, he could feel his heartbeat begin to slow. Stefan's wrath doubled, his rage expanded until it exploded within him.

The next thing he knew, he was lying on a floor of stones. Stefan rose up on his arm and looked around for Ilinca so he could kill the gypsy witch.

Except there was nothing but darkness and silence.

The silence was eerie and the dark was cold, malicious.

He managed to get to his knees before he grew dizzy. He fell forward onto his hands and took huge gulps of breath.

"You're here, Stefan Kennedy, because you are empty inside," said a female voice all around him, crackling with age. "For that I curse you. You will be locked in this place until you get the chance to control your rage. If you fail, you'll spend eternity here."

Stefan sat back on his haunches with his hands on his thighs. It looked like he would never get out of whatever hell the old gypsy had put him in.

That thought only made his fury grow.

He got to his feet and felt...nothing. There

wasn't even a stirring of air. No cold, no heat, no sound, and definitely no light. He wasn't thirsty or hungry or tired.

What he was, however, was totally and completely alone.

Stefan knew that feeling well. It hadn't been around in a decade, but it was familiar nonetheless. It had remained his constant companion after his mother had died, right up until Ronan, Morcant, and Daman befriended him.

Where were his friends? Ronan and Morcant had disappeared in front of him. Did that mean Ilinca cursed them, as well? Could they be in this same prison?

Stefan grunted. "No' likely."

Ilinca wouldn't be so kind as to put all four of them in the same place, not where they might find each other. As for Daman, Stefan knew his friend was most likely cursed, as well.

Something snapped inside Stefan. It was the part of him that his friends kept in check, the part that fell away after his mother had died.

This time he knew it was gone for good, and he welcomed the anger as he began to plan how he would kill Ilinca.

CHAPTER ONE

Highlands, 1609

Morvan exited her home and looked to the morning sky as she stretched. There was a nip in the air, a hint that autumn would soon arrive. She surveyed the wooded landscape around her and sighed with pleasure. There was nowhere else she would rather live. The trees helped to cut the wind during the harsh winters, but that's not why she preferred the forest.

Some called her magical.

Others called her cursed.

All Morvan knew, was that the forest was her home. She understood the plants and animals. If that made her cursed, then she would gladly accept the mantle.

She combed her fingers through her hair to push the heavy length out of her face, then quickly plaited it and tied it off with a strip of leather.

"What is in store for me today?" she asked, her steps light and eager as she walked the short distance to the loch.

The mountain was steep in places and the rocks many as she made her way down to the water. She stopped just before she left the trees when she saw a herd of red deer drinking on the opposite bank of the narrow strip of water.

Morvan waited, taking in the sight of the impressive herd. They knew her scent, but she didn't want to intrude. It wasn't until the last of them had had their fill and trotted away that she continued to the loch.

She sat against a grouping of rocks and pulled an oatcake out of her pocket. It was rare for her not to be at the loch first thing in the morning. As she ate her breakfast, Morvan contemplated the day.

Normally, there was a set area she would walk looking for animals that were in need of healing. Though the village thought her touched, there were those who didn't hesitate to ask for her skills if one of their animals were sick.

The day before had been spent at the miller's tending to the injured hoof of one of his sheep. Perhaps it was that she had been kept from the woods by helping the miller that she felt the need to just wander the forest and see what she could find.

With the oatcake finished, Morvan dusted off her hands and got to her feet. She turned to the right and began walking. As soon as she stepped back into the woods, a shiver ran down her spine. She halted instantly. The forest had been her home all her life, and not once had she ever felt such...foreboding. As if fate were warning her that something was coming.

Or was already there.

Morvan touched the nearest tree, a tall evergreen. The bark scraped her palm and pine needles crunched beneath her feet. The smell of pine permeated the air.

"What is it?" she asked the tree.

She didn't expect an answer, but since she lived alone, she found it better to talk to the plants and animals rather than not talk at all.

Morvan took a deep breath as the music of the forest assaulted her. The wind whistling through the leaves, the creak of the limbs, the sweet songs of birds. Every animal, every plant contributed to the beautiful music.

When Morvan was just a child, she'd discovered that she was the only one who could hear the melody. She let her hand trail down the trunk of the tree as she lifted her foot and took a step. Then another, and another.

There wasn't another chill, but she still couldn't shake the feeling that something was going to happen. It didn't make her turn around though. Morvan didn't turn away from anything or anyone. She slowly walked through the forest, stopping every now and again to admire a bird or flower.

It didn't take long for her to relax as the tranquility of the woods seeped into her. She lost herself in the forest. She was spellbound by the serenity, enthralled by the peacefulness.

Morvan suddenly stopped and looked around. She knew every inch of the woods – especially the boundary between the MacKay's lands and those of clan Sinclair that she was never to cross.

How then had she crossed the border?

With her heart pounding, Morvan hastily glanced around to make sure no one was hiding in the foliage. She took a tentative step back, appalled to realize she was much farther onto Sinclair land than she'd first thought.

Morvan swallowed nervously. Tensions between the Sinclairs and her clan, the MacKays, were high, especially after a recent skirmish. The last time she was in the village near the keep, she'd heard that there was trouble within the castle. The new laird, Alistair, was bent on peace while his younger brother Donald, still upset over not becoming laird, wanted war.

She didn't want to be responsible for starting the war simply because she'd crossed the boundary by accident. It was so stupid of her. She knew better. No matter how many times she gave herself up to the woods, she had never ventured off her clan's land. Ever.

From the moment she'd woken that morning, she'd felt as if there were something particularly different about the day, something not quite normal. Morvan hadn't questioned it further though, and that's apparently where she went wrong. She should've remained in her cottage.

Morvan spun around and walked back toward her clan's land as fast and quietly as she could. She didn't know this side of the forest like she did her own, and it complicated things. Twice, she had to retrace her steps and take a different route. Sweat beaded her forehead as she lifted her skirts to free her legs in an attempt to move faster.

It was a distressed bleating that brought her to a halt a second time. Morvan closed her eyes and sighed. There was an injured animal calling to her for help. But the longer she remained on Sinclair land, the more she put herself and her clan in peril.

Her shoulders slumped even as she turned toward the sound. No amount of danger could keep her from helping an animal in need.

Morvan followed the cries, recognizing them as being from a red deer. A few moments later, she moved aside foliage and caught sight of the majestic buck that had his impressive antlers tangled in the branches of a tree.

The buck caught her scent before he saw her, and it set him to jerking his antlers in a renewed attempt to get free. Morvan began to hum softly and walked toward the frightened animal. The louder the buck cried, the more his hooves flailed and his legs kicked, she louder she hummed, all the while moving slowly and calmly.

She slowed and cocked her head to the side when she caught the buck's gaze. "Easy now, handsome. I'm here to help."

The buck let out a snort, his black eyes wild with fatigue and fear. Morvan remained where she was, hoping the animal would calm a bit to allow her to get closer.

The humming helped, but she had to touch him before she could really help him. The longer she waited, the more the buck's frenzy would double. By the marks on the tree from his antlers, and the grooves in the ground from his pawing of the earth, the poor animal had been stuck for some time.

With only five feet separating them, Morvan took a deep breath and moved closer. As soon as she did, the buck kicked out a hoof. Morvan grunted as it slammed into her stomach, knocking her backwards.

She clutched her abdomen but kept eye contact with the buck. Pushing past the pain, Morvan once more walked to the deer. He kicked her twice more in the legs before she was finally able to put a hand on his flank.

Instantly, the animal calmed. Tears gathered when she felt how the buck shook beneath her palm. She hummed and softly stroked him while walking around to his other side.

"It's all right now. I'm here to get you loose," she whispered in a sing-song voice that matched the tune she was humming.

The buck closed his eyes. Morvan ran her hand up to his spine, then forward to where his antlers sprouted from his head. She kept one hand on him at all times and slowly turned his head this way and that to get him free.

For the next ten minutes she worked, sweat dripping down her face. The buck's breathing had calmed, but he needed food and water quickly.

Suddenly, the thick antlers came free. Morvan released the animal as he stumbled backwards a few steps. His black soulful eyes blinked at her for a heartbeat. Then he walked to her and lowered his head enough so that she could rub his forehead.

"You're welcome," she whispered with a smile. "Go now. The forest is calling to you."

The buck turned and leapt over a fallen tree before he bounded out of sight. No matter how many animals she saved, their gratitude afterwards always made her teary.

Morvan leaned against a tree and gently touched her stomach, knee and shin where the deer had kicked her. She was lucky not to have any broken bones, but there was definitely going to be bruising. Despite the injuries she'd sustained, it was worth it to save an animal.

She turned east to return to MacKay land and had only gone a few steps when something urged her to go left. Morvan tried to fight the compulsion, but the force was too strong. Trepidation made her hands clammy. Four times she tried to turn around, and each time the force compelling her grew stronger.

Morvan gave up fighting and allowed the compulsion to take her where it would. To her horror, she walked deeper onto Sinclair land toward a rock structure that seemed to burst out of the ground and stretch to the heavens. Every step she took left a sinking feeling of doom that spread through her.

Quickly, she found herself at the structure, staring up. Morvan tried to turn around, but the force wouldn't loosen its hold. With a sigh, she began to climb up a steep incline riddled with moss-coated rocks. By the time she reached the top, she was winded and weary. Precipitation began to fall in a soft drizzle that quickly increased. Morvan blinked through the rain.

All around her were massive boulders that dwarfed her. Morvan saw an opening to a cave and dashed. She didn't know where to go next. The feeling that had been guiding her was gone. She hoped that meant she'd reached her destination, but as far as she could tell, there was no animal for her to help.

"Which means what, exactly?" she mumbled in frustration.

Not only was she on Sinclair land, but she was also miles away from her woods. She wished she were back in her cottage sipping a mug of tea.

Morvan poked her head out of the cave and lifted her face to the sky but saw nothing but gray. The storm could be over in a moment, or it could linger for hours. She didn't like the idea of climbing back down the slope, especially after the rain had made the damp stones slick. But she couldn't remain there anymore either.

Morvan glanced over her shoulder to the dark

cave behind her. She didn't know how far back it went, or what might be living inside, and she didn't want to find out.

A look out of the cave once more revealed boulders that almost looked as if they were placed in a maze-like pattern. But that couldn't possibly be right. No one but giants could lift those boulders, and there were no giants.

The atmosphere suddenly became ominous, foreboding. It wasn't the weather, but...almost as if a dark presence were causing the shift. There was no denying the malevolence, the cruelty permeating the very air.

Morvan didn't like the place. She wanted to get as far from it as she could.

With no weapon in sight, she walked out from the shelter of the cave and went back the way she had come to return to her cottage. Only it was blocked by a boulder. A boulder that hadn't been there before.

Magic. Her mind voiced the word she wasn't prepared to let past her lips.

Morvan looked up at the rock that seemed to reach the heavens. She tried to find a way around it, but both sides were melded into the rock on either side of it leaving her walled in. She spun around and faced the narrow path between the other rocks. If she wanted to leave, she was going to have to walk the trail.

Her heart thumped a slow, dreadful beat in her chest. The first step was the hardest. With every one after, she expected something to jump out at her from behind one of the boulders. She heard something behind her, but when she tried to turn around and see what it was, a voice in her head screamed for her not to. Morvan wisely kept her gaze ahead of her.

The path led her on a continual soft incline this way and that. Normally she knew her way instinctively, but she was so turned around that she didn't know if she would ever find home again.

The rain was at least letting up enough so she could see a little ways ahead of her. That was how she saw the wall of rock. It towered before her, carved with thousands of markings of various sizes.

As a child of the woods, Morvan kept her Celtic roots close. She recognized the carvings as those of the Celts. By their worn look, these were ancient. It was as if the wall was important to the Celts. Why else would they carve all of these symbols into it? There was also a slight humming coming from the stone, as if it were alive.

Magic, her mind whispered again.

Magic had brought her to the cliff, and magic filled the air. Why had it chosen her? That dark feeling from earlier was now gone. It had dissipated after she'd left the cave. Morvan began to wonder if there were some kind of entity guiding her. It made her shiver with fear – and wonder.

No matter how many times she looked at the ancient Celtic symbols, she kept coming back to a carving of a wolf. The carving was larger than her hand, the knotwork exquisite.

She knew the wolf could be literal or symbolic.

And it could mean any number of things. The Old Ways taught her that a man marked with the symbol of the wolf was fearless, brave, and rarely compromised. They were the men who became heroes in the heat of battle. They would not back down, and they would take no quarter. They thrived on challenges. Their character was impeccable, and they lived by a creed of honor.

What did that mean for her, however? There were a few instances in history when a woman was marked with a wolf, but those times were rare. Besides, Morvan knew her place. She was anything but a wolf.

She stared at the etching for long moments. Another overwhelming feeling filled her. This time, she felt the need to touch the wolf etching, to run her fingers over it. She didn't know why it was so important.

Or why she hesitated.

Morvan swallowed and gave in to the need. As soon as her fingertip came in contact with the symbol, there was a loud boom, and a gust of air from the stone that sent her flying backwards.

CHAPTER TWO

One moment Stefan was encased in darkness, and the next he was standing in the rain. He didn't stop to wonder why he was out of his prison. He ducked behind the first stone he saw, crouched down, and looked around for an enemy.

His hunt had begun. It was the same hunt he swore he would take if he ever got out of the hellish place Ilinca had put him in. The gypsy would pay for what she had done to him and his friends. All Stefan had thought about was the gypsy's death, of how he would take her last breath. Until the old woman was dead, he couldn't rest, couldn't think about his friends.

He pushed his long, wet hair out of his face and stood. He needed to know where he was. Stefan climbed atop the boulder and surveyed the area.

There was nothing about the forest that looked familiar, but he recognized the trees and the mist-covered mountains. He was still in Scotland, and that meant it was only a matter of time before he found the gypsy.

Stefan leapt to the ground, landing with bent knees. He wouldn't put it past Ilinca to send someone after him, but the old woman had no idea who she'd put into that darkness. If she thought he had nothing but anger in his heart before, now it consumed him.

He went from boulder to boulder. There was someone up ahead. He could hear their breathing as well as a grunt of pain. Stefan lifted his lips in a sneer. So, Ilinca hadn't taken long to send her first assassin.

Stefan rushed from behind the boulder. He didn't have a weapon, but with the fury inside him, his hands would be enough. Just as he rounded the next rock, he saw a tangle of dark skirts as a woman used a boulder to get to her feet. Woman or man, it didn't matter. Anyone sent by Ilinca would die.

Then the woman turned to face him and he saw her arresting face. That one moment of hesitation surprised him as much as it did her. But Stefan was already on a collision course, and there was no time to alter his direction.

Time slowed, allowing him to see her nutmeg brown eyes widen and her lips part in surprise. Stefan managed to slow himself, but it wasn't enough. The woman stepped back to get out of his way, only there was nothing behind her. Her arms flailed, and those big eyes of hers filled with panic. Then she was gone.

Stefan slid to a stop, one foot going over the side of the cliff as dirt and pebbles followed the woman down. He leaned over the side and spied the body amid the thick ferns and jagged rocks below.

He wanted to forget the woman, but he couldn't. It wasn't just her eyes, it was her face. Creamy skin unblemished except for a small, dark mole at the corner of her right eye. Inky black brows that matched her long braid gently arching over her eyes. High cheekbones and full lips made for kissing.

The woman wasn't Romany. Her skin wasn't nearly dark enough, but that didn't mean she hadn't been sent by Ilinca.

Stefan stared down at the unmoving form of the woman for long moments. She was most likely dead anyway. The odds of her missing any of the rocks were slim. Besides, he had a gypsy to kill.

~ ~ ~

Pain, ferocious and intense, roughly dragged Morvan awake. She inhaled, and then wished she hadn't as agony reverberated through her. She was afraid to move and make the pain worse. Yet she couldn't remain where she was.

Drops of water fell on her face. Morvan opened her eyes and looked at the sky, blinking from the rain that had slackened to a light drizzle.

She wiggled her toes, thankful that it seemed nothing was wrong with her legs. Next she moved her fingers, again feeling nothing amiss with her upper body other than her ribs. Gingerly, she rolled onto her side, gasping at the pain. It took several attempts before she was able to move to her hands and knees. That's when her arm began to throb.

Morvan looked at her left arm, but there was no tear in her dress or any blood. She could move her arm, so she didn't suspect it was broken. Her ribs, however, already bruised from the buck's kick, were the worst of everything.

Keeping her breathing light, Morvan eventually made it to her feet. Then wished she hadn't when she grew dizzy. She was able to grab hold of a tree growing between two rocks to steady herself. She stood silently for several moments waiting for the world to stop spinning. Morvan closed her eyes and evened her breathing. That's when she recalled the man.

He'd looked as wild and untamed as the animals in the forest. His eyes, a stunning hazel mix of blue, green, and gold, were stony and feral. Half of his face was hidden by his long, light brown hair.

But it was his lips formed in a cold, hard line that frightened her most of all.

There was no compassion in the man, no kindness or gentleness. He'd shown that when he hadn't tried to help her when she'd lost her balance. The fact he also hadn't come down to see if she were alive or dead spoke volumes.

It reminded Morvan why she chose the forest and animals over the village and the people within. She understood animals and their behavior, but people she could never fully grasp. One of her downfalls was believing people spoke honestly, when in fact they never did.

Animals didn't lie or deceive. Animals didn't betray or manipulate. They didn't exploit or abuse, steal or cheat.

Morvan opened her eyes and held her sore left arm against her battered ribs. It was going to be a long walk home.

~ ~ ~

Stefan circled the area to get an idea of any potential threats, but all he found was the woman. To his amazement, she was on her feet, though she looked the worse for wear. Her skin was pale, and by the way she held her left arm, she was injured. Yet the woman didn't shout for help or wait for someone to find her. She began walking.

Stefan once more chose to ignore the female. She was alive, and apparently knew where she was going. He, on the other hand, had hunting to do.

Ilinca.

He had no idea how many days had passed while he paced and fumed inside the darkness where she had confined him, but it didn't matter. Whether it had been a few days or several years, he would find the gypsy.

There was no holding back his fury – nor did he

want to. He fed the rage, nurtured the wrath until every bit of gentleness and humanity his friends cultivated in him vanished.

He was the monster his mother feared he would become.

He was his father.

Stefan used to fear he would become his father, but now he embraced his lineage, welcomed it with open arms. It would be what freed his friends. It would be what helped him kill Ilinca and break whatever magic she'd used to put him in that dark hell.

By then he would be too far gone to ever be among people again. But it was a price he would gladly pay once he knew Morcant, Daman, and Ronan were liberated from Ilinca.

Stefan didn't walk the forest. He stalked, he hunted. He moved as quickly as a hare, as silently as a hawk, and as deadly as a wolf.

The farther he went from the stone cliff, the sharper his senses became. He didn't care how long it took him to find Ilinca, he wouldn't stop. If he had to walk the length and breadth of Scotland a hundred times over, he would do it. Nothing and no one would stop him from his mission.

The gypsy took him from the only family he had, the brothers who kept him from giving in to the monster inside him. For that, she would pay with her life.

Stefan paused when he heard water. It seemed like eons since he'd heard such a sound. It was...musical. Unable to forget it, he shifted from his path and went towards the sound of the flowing water. When he reached the stream, he simply stared.

The rain stopped and the clouds parted long enough for a ray of sunlight to shine upon the water. The glint of the light off the surface made it appear golden, and caused Stefan to raise his hands to shield his eyes from the brightness.

Suddenly, he found his mouth dry. He was so thirsty. He took stock of everything before he walked to the stream and knelt beside it. Stefan cupped his hand and brought handful after handful of water to his mouth.

When he was satisfied, he took in the majestic view of the mountains rising all around him. Even with the gray sky, there was nothing more beautiful than the Highlands.

It made him think of his friends. They were the only reason he was sane enough to recall their names. It saddened him that he would never be able to talk to them again. He didn't want them to see what he had become. All three would try and change him, and they would never stop.

But there was no changing him back to what he was. The monster was loose. The anger had become a living, breathing thing inside him that nothing could defeat.

This was how his life was always meant to turn out. His mother had tried to change his future, but there was only so much she could do once his father refused to acknowledge Stefan's existence.

Just thinking of his father sent a wave of fury

rumbling through him. Stefan could still remember his father's stony look, his callous laughter when Stefan was six and ran away from his mother to go to his father.

That's the day he learned he was a bastard. It was the day the monster inside him was born.

It was also the day he learned the only person in the whole world who cared about him was his mother. She tried to help him control his anger, anger that was passed from his father onto him. If not for his mother, Stefan would've been lost to his monster, just as his father had succumbed to his.

For the next ten years, it was just Stefan and his mother. Then his mother died suddenly. Stefan had been terrified of the anger inside him, but there wasn't fear now. Now, he embraced it.

He rose to his feet and started back to the trees when a sound to his right drew his attention. His head jerked around and he saw the woman from earlier stumble out of the forest to the stream.

Stefan hid behind a tree and watched her. She had leaves sticking out of her braid, or what hair remained in the plait anyway. Her gown had patches of mud and dirt on it. After she drank, she wrung out the water from her skirts and hung her head.

As she sat there, Stefan was shocked to see a buck walk up to her. When the buck lowered his head, Stefan thought the deer might attack her. To his surprise, the buck pawed the earth as if to get her attention.

When the woman lifted her head, she looked at

the deer and smiled. He couldn't tell what she said from the distance, but she was talking to the buck. Stefan grew more confused when the woman draped an arm around the deer's neck and it helped her back to her feet.

Stefan shook his head and turned away. There were still several hours of daylight left. He walked another ten minutes before he found a road that cut through the forest.

He remained hidden as a man on horseback rode past. Stefan took note of the plaid and the sword the man carried. It didn't take long for Stefan to decide to follow the man even though it took him back in the direction he had come from.

Stefan hadn't been following the rider long when the man drew his mount to a stop and simply sat there. Stefan couldn't see the man's face because of his cloak and hood, but the man was being cautious. A moment later, he clicked the horse back into a walk.

Stefan was glad of his decision to follow the rider when they came to a castle. He recognized the preparations taking place. With all the activity, it was apparent the clan was gearing for war. He took note of the number of warriors this clan held.

Stefan crept closer to the castle and overheard someone mention the name Sinclair. If he was on Sinclair land, then that meant he was only a hundred miles or so from where he was last with his friends.

He turned and made his way back to the forest. Now that he knew where he was, he knew which

direction he needed to go. Which was where he had
been headed to begin with.

Stefan easily made up the time he'd lost by
following the man. He found the stream again and
kept going, running low and fast. As the sun began
to set, he crested a hill and saw smoke curling from
the trees. Hunger rumbled in his stomach and he
decided to check it out.

Surprise ripped through him when he found a
small cottage and the same woman from the cliff.
Instead of being inside tending to her wounds, she
was feeding the chickens while barely keeping on
her feet. It was while she tried to bring in more
wood that she collapsed.

Stefan waited a few moments to see if she
would wake. When she didn't, he walked from the
trees and squatted beside her. He moved aside the
black hair that had fallen over her face to look at
her.

Why had she been so far from her home? What
had she been doing on that cliff?

He didn't want those questions running
through his mind, and he certainly didn't want the
answers. He stood, intending to turn away when he
recalled her face up on the cliff right before she
fell. He had no idea how he'd gotten on the cliff,
and there was a chance something similar had
happened to her.

A sliver of emotion churned in his gut. He felt
responsible for her injuries. That's the only reason
he bent and gathered her in his arms and stood. He
kicked the door to the cottage open and walked

inside to the bed before he set her down. As he pulled his arms from beneath her, his hand touched her skin and he felt the coolness.

If the lass could live after such a fall and make the trek all the way to the cottage, fate had a plan for her. That's the only reason Stefan hurriedly removed her wet boots, stockings, gown, and shift.

As he was pulling the blanket over her, he spotted the huge bruise covering her left side. Stefan tucked the blanket tight, threw a log onto her dying fire and walked out, intending to forget her.

CHAPTER THREE

Morvan was on her side when she woke. She opened her eyes and looked into the flames in the hearth. The last thing she remembered was trying to get more wood to stoke the fire. When had she gotten it? More importantly, when did she get undressed and into bed?

She clutched her side and slowly sat up, realizing she was naked. Something was definitely wrong because she never went to bed naked.

Morvan wrapped the blanket around her and stood to walk to the window. She looked out the shutter to see the faint glow of the sun just breaking over the mountain. Her stomach rumbled loudly. She turned away from the window and walked to the table where she cut a piece of bread and added a slice of cold ham to it. Morvan ate four pieces of ham and two portions of bread before she retrieved a clean gown and petticoat. Her boots and stockings also in her arms, she walked from the cottage.

She had never walked down to the loch in nothing but a blanket, but there was no one about to see or disturb her, so Morvan didn't worry. She was more concerned with the missing hours she couldn't remember.

Had she fallen so hard that she would lose time? Surely if that were to happen, it would've happened right after she woke from the fall off the cliff. She hadn't hit her head on any rocks, but that didn't mean her brain hadn't been addled a bit by such a rough tumble.

When Morvan reached the loch, she draped her clean clothes over a low-hanging branch along with the blanket. Then she walked into the water. It was cool against her skin, making her catch her breath at the contact. When the water reached her hips, she dove under, remaining beneath until her lungs began to burn.

When she surfaced, she played in the water for a bit, trying to relax after the day before. It wasn't just her injuries or the fall, it was the fact she had been on Sinclair land for a long time. As far as she knew, none of the MacKays had seen her, but she also didn't want to go into the village and find out if she was wrong.

Morvan gathered sand from the bottom of the loch and began to wash. She was so out of sorts that she'd forgotten her soap at the cottage. When she finished, she walked to the shore and wrung out her hair.

It wasn't until she was walking back to her clothes that she had the suspicion someone was watching her, which was ridiculous. No one would want to spy on her.

She used the blanket to dry off and then hurriedly dressed. Only then did she look around, but she could find no indication that anyone was there.

"I'm just rattled," she murmured.

That had to be the excuse. After the man had come out of nowhere on top of the cliff and she'd fallen, she hadn't been the same. Well, that wasn't exactly true. It had begun yesterday morning. She still couldn't pinpoint exactly what it was, but everything about the day before had been a little off.

Morvan gathered the blanket and made her way back to the cottage. She needed to mix some herbs to help with the pain of her ribs, not to mention a poultice to deal with the ugly bruising.

Once inside, she made the tea and added some herbs for the pain. While she drank the mixture, she combed out her hair, which proved difficult with her ribs. When the tangles were all out, she left her hair free and ventured back into the woods to look for the herbs she would need for the poultice.

If she had been thinking clearly yesterday after she'd helped the buck, she would have gathered them then. She'd used her last bit on the blacksmith's horse two days earlier when it had come up with a lame leg.

Morvan brought some oatcakes with her since she was still hungry from missing two meals the day before. She wasn't twenty steps from her cottage when she found a hare caught in a trap.

She looked around because she hadn't set the trap. Someone else had. Someone else who had been close to her cottage. Morvan bent and touched the frightened hare. The animal instantly stopped fighting and stayed calm as she removed the vine from its hind leg.

"Off you go," she said and watched it hop away.

It wasn't that she minded someone hunting. Everyone had to eat. What disturbed her was that it had been done so close to her cottage, and she hadn't even known about it.

Out of the corner of her eye, Morvan saw movement. She jerked around, but there was nothing but a fern leaf swaying. Before she could react to whatever was out there, she heard a group of men stomping through the forest. The fact that the sound was coming from the direction of her laird's castle meant that her clan was probably marching off to war.

Morvan quickly hid behind a large oak and plastered her back to the bark. The men were getting closer. They were talking in low tones, but the mood was dark and dangerous. She didn't want them finding her because her clan or not, she wasn't exactly welcome.

Men on their way to battle were likely to do all sorts of things to a woman alone. If everything she knew about her clan were true, then it was only the roughest, meanest warriors who remained.

Suddenly, there was a shout from one of the men. Everything went silent for a heartbeat, and then chaos erupted. There was no clang of swords, yet there was no denying the sounds of battle. The shouts of pain, the bellows of outrage, and the grunts of the dying could clearly be heard.

Had the Sinclairs ambushed her clan?

Morvan glanced around the tree and saw her clan. And one man attacking them. She gaped in astonishment that one man could do such damage to a group of fifteen men. He was quick and agile, swift and lethal. He used no sword, just his hands and a dagger.

As the man pivoted away, she caught a glimpse of his face. It was the same man from the cliff. She was mesmerized, captivated.

Six of her clansman left alive ran back the way they had come as the man fought a seventh. She covered her mouth with her hand as her clansman fell. The man from the cliff stood among the dead breathing heavily. He started to turn away when one of the six who'd run off returned and threw a dagger that landed in the man's thigh.

The stranger's face turned deadly, as feral as a wild animal's when he locked his gaze on his attacker. In quick order, he had her clansman in his grip, and the man died quickly and violently.

Morvan knew she couldn't be seen by the man.

Even as he staggered and slammed against a tree, she knew she had to leave. She waited until he pulled the dagger from his thigh before she took a step back. She held her breath when her foot landed on a stick and it split, the sound as loud as a crack of thunder in the silence of the forest.

The man's head jerked around to her and their gazes locked. He pushed away from the tree, and she saw the blood seeping from various wounds on his arms and chest. Though his eyes were wild and focused, his body wasn't responding as it had before. He took two steps toward her before he went down on one knee.

He growled, his face twisted with anger – at her or himself for not rising, she didn't know. Her heart ached as she watched him try to get up. It reminded her of the elk she'd seen be taken down by an arrow the winter before. The massive animal had fought the death that awaited it, it struggled and scraped to get its legs underneath it, only to stagger a few steps and fall back down.

Which was exactly what the stranger was doing.

Morvan couldn't stand to see any animal suffer – even a man. At the same time, the stranger was still in the grips of battle. He wouldn't stop until she was dead.

She lifted her skirts and started running. Even with her heart pounding and her breath rushing, she could hear him behind her. The only thing in her favor was the fact that she knew this forest better than anyone. She ran in the opposite direction from her cottage, her gaze directly in front of her to the stream. There was no use looking behind her. All her concentration was needed to maneuver around trees and rocks.

She could hear him closing in, knew he was about to grab her. Morvan caught a glimpse of the stream through the trees. She was so close. All she had to do was get him to the water. She knew where the shallow spots were. If he fell into the deep part, it would give her time to get away.

Morvan shrieked when her head was jerked back as the man grabbed the ends of her hair. She swatted her arm behind her and connected with him. It was all that was needed to get him to release her.

With renewed drive, she pumped her legs faster. A smile formed when she came to the stream and headed for the shallow part. Luck was on her side as her boot hit the shore of the water.

Suddenly, she was slammed into from behind. The water came at her quickly, and then she was on her back looking into hazel eyes. She watched, confused, as his anger faded and clarity filled his eyes.

He kept her from going under the water by shifting, his hold easing considerably. With his chest heaving, he frowned down at her. Blood gushed from his wounds, and he blinked, fighting to stay conscious.

A tremor went through him as he released her and fell back. Morvan warily sat up and discovered the stranger had passed out. If any of the MacKays arrived and found him, they would kill him instantly. She should want his death, and yet, the same feeling that urged her to the cliff the day before screamed at her to heal the man.

She might live on MacKay land, but she didn't consider them her clan. She didn't have a clan. The forest was her home, the animals within it her family. So she didn't feel as if she were betraying a clan who didn't want her.

Morvan stood in the water and looked around to find a secluded section where she could hide the stranger. Using the water to help, she pulled him to the spot she'd selected. It took awhile between his weight, her ribs, and her heavy skirts to pull him as far out of the water as she could.

Then she rushed around finding the herbs she needed to staunch the bleeding. She packed the leaves and flower petals into the wounds and tore off strips of her shift to bind them in place.

When she finished the last one, she sat back and looked at the man. He was tall and muscular, a Highlander in every sense of the word. Never had she seen someone kill with their bare hands, but that's exactly what he had done – to ten men.

Morvan looked down at her hands to see the blood upon them. She rinsed her hands in the water as she took in the man's face. His face was all hard angles, but with his hollowed cheeks and full bottom lip, he was striking.

Unable to resist, she ran the back of her fingers along his cheek and then sank her fingers into his thick hair. His deep brown eyebrows were a shade darker than his hair and slashed over his eyes.

Now that his forehead was no longer furrowed, he looked younger and much calmer.

"Who are you?" she whispered.

He slept on, unaware of her question. That was just one of many she had, however. She hoped he would wake in time to answer them, but she doubted he was the kind of man who would give answers if he didn't want to.

Her world of solitude and silence had been shattered, and there was nothing she could do about it. There was a possibility her clansmen wouldn't come to her cottage. It was a slim one. At least the stranger had a chance to escape. If he woke in time.

Somehow, she didn't think he was the kind of man to lie around no matter how severe the wound. No, he would be up and gone as soon as he woke. Which was probably a good thing.

Morvan sighed. Besides stitching them, she had done all she could for his wounds. It was too bad he wasn't awake. She found herself wanting to hear his voice to see if it matched the virile, muscular visage of the man she had witnessed in the heat of battle.

Then again, she would be better served getting as far from him as she could.

CHAPTER FOUR

Stefan's eyes snapped open to see thick, puffy clouds lazily drifting across a blue sky. He felt like roasted arse and he didn't know why his feet were wet inside his boots.

He raised his head and saw the stream, and then he remembered the woman. He recalled his anger directed at her. He'd grabbed her, and it was like a veil had been lifted from him. Everything became calm and clear for a moment.

The same had happened the night before when he'd carried her into her cottage, but he hadn't realized it until they were in the water.

Stefan couldn't recall what had happened after touching the woman, or before he was chasing her through the forest. Why had he chased her? It was the same woman from the cliff, and the same woman he'd watched swim in the loch that morning. But that shouldn't have made him go after her.

He ran a hand down his face and sat up, grimacing at the pain that assaulted him from his chest, arms, and thigh. Someone had tended to his wounds, and if the material binding him were any indication, it was the woman.

If she'd run from him, it was because she was frightened. Why would she then tend to him?

There was only one way to find out.

Stefan started to get to his feet when he heard a snap of a limb. He slowly pulled his boots out of the water and turned so he could look over the foliage covering him when he saw six men, all wearing blue and green tartans.

"Find him," demanded the tallest of the men. He carried a sword in his meaty fist, a look of rage contorting his face.

Stefan remained hidden as he watched the men follow tracks to the stream. They waded across and began looking for another trail.

"The tracks stop, Donald," one of the men said to the leader.

Donald's gaze looked up and down the stream, pausing for a moment near where Stefan hid. "We tracked him this far, we can find his trail again. The bastard will pay for killing our clansmen."

Stefan might have holes in his memory, but his wounds combined with the fact that he woke at the stream made it a safe bet that he was who the men were looking for. The longer he remained, the sooner they would find him. Stefan waited until the group – minus the leader - were out of sight up stream before he decided to go in the opposite direction. He kept bent over and had only taken one step when voices reached him.

"Look who we found," came a man's voice full of laughter.

Stefan paused, though he wasn't sure why.

"Were you here?" Donald demanded.

A feminine voice said, "I'm always here. The forest is my home."

Stefan looked over his shoulders and saw the woman, her black hair in a neat braid as she held Donald's gaze with her chin high.

She was brave and fearless despite one man towering over her, and another behind her holding both of her arms. It was the perfect time for Stefan to get away. Why then did he remain?

"I hear the whispers of you," Donald said in a hard voice, his lip lifted in a sneer. "You and your magic."

"I don't have magic," the woman protested.

Donald gave a snort. "I could have you burned. Tell me what I want to know, and I'll leave you alone."

"I have no magic," she said again through clenched teeth.

A third man walked around the group and stopped at the water's edge. He looked back and said, "Donald, Morvan is known as a healer of sorts. Perhaps she was...unaware...that she was helping a man who is an enemy to us."

Donald regarded Morvan for a moment. "Did you find a stranger and heal him?"

Stefan's gaze was glued to Morvan. It was an unusual name for a particularly unusual woman. He used the group's diverted attention to steadily move away from his hiding spot and into the forest, careful that he didn't encounter any more men.

Stefan didn't stop until he was on the other side of the group, and then he crouched down behind a pine. It brought him closer to Morvan, and to his dismay, he was drawn to her in a way he couldn't explain.

No matter how he tried, he couldn't shake the feeling that he was meant to be there to help her.

"Tell me true, Morvan," Donald said. "He killed your clansman. He needs to be caught and punished."

For long moments, Morvan held Donald's gaze. Then she finally said, "Aye, I came upon a man and tended him."

"Where?" Donald asked tightly.

Morvan pointed to where Stefan had been. While the leader and one of his men went to look, Morvan was held in place by the guard.

Stefan waited until Donald and his man were nearly to where Morvan had left him before he came out from behind the tree. He kicked Morvan's guard in the back of the knee, dropping him down while snapping the man's neck.

Morvan twisted away and turned to gape at him. "You should be gone," she whispered urgently.

There wasn't time for Stefan to respond as a shout from across the stream brought the leader's attention to them. Stefan grabbed Morvan's hand - feeling the same calming sensation he recognized from before – and jerked her behind him.

Her brown eyes were wide with fear, but she didn't argue. Stefan took a deep breath and faced his attackers.

~ ~ ~

For the second time that day, Morvan watched the stranger battle. As injured as he was, he moved as if he didn't feel anything, as if he hadn't lost all that blood.

The man she faced a moment ago wasn't the same one who had chased her earlier. The clarity was still there, but for how long? As MacKay men came at him, she saw the bloodlust take him again. At least that's what she thought at first.

The more he fought, the more she saw the anger return. It was like it consumed him, took him. The more the men came at him, the more the fury showed. One by one, the men of her clan died by the stranger's hand. It wasn't until he was battling Donald that she knew she had to stop him.

Morvan shouted, hoping to get the stranger's attention. When that didn't work, she walked closer. "You must stop," she said. "There has been enough killing."

She stepped over the fallen men as Donald and the stranger punched each other. The stranger had divested Donald of his sword early on in the fight, and it was all hand-to-hand now.

Suddenly, the stranger had Donald on his back, choking him. Morvan hurried to the men, knowing that the stranger might very well turn on her again.

"Stop," she said and touched him.

Just as before, she felt a tremor go through him. He didn't release Donald, but he loosened his grip and turned his head toward her.

"No more killing," she said again and looked into the man's hazel eyes. Morvan glanced down at Donald to find him watching them.

The man looked back at Donald and slammed his fist into Donald's jaw, knocking him out. The man then got to his feet and faced her.

"You can no' go back," he stated.

His voice was as deep and silky as she imagined it would be. It sent a thrill through her that clumped low in her belly, urging her to take note of his fierceness – as well as his protection of her.

The lucidity had returned to the man again. Had her touch done that? In animals yes, but she hadn't known it to work on humans. Then again, he was more beast than man when in battle.

"Did you no' hear me, lass? Donald knows you've helped me. Twice, I might add. He'll kill you."

Morvan glanced back in the direction of her cottage. "No one knows this forest like I do."

"He'll find you eventually. Come with me," he urged.

She looked down at the hand he held out to

her. "I don't even know your name."

"It's Stefan. Stefan Kennedy."

"Where are we going?" she asked as she took his hand and he led her towards the water.

"As far from here as we can get. Is there another clan who will take you in?"

Since their only option was to cross the stream, Morvan lead him to the shallow part when she drew up at his words. "What? I thought you were from the Sinclairs."

"Nay. My clan is far from here."

The day was growing grimmer by the moment. Morvan crossed the stream, but as soon as they were on the other side, Stefan took the lead.

"How far is it to Sinclair land?"

"Not far," she said staring at his back. There was more blood on him, and she would guess that his other wounds were bleeding again. "We should reach the border in about thirty minutes."

He held a tree limb up for her to duck under. "Do you know anyone there?"

"Nay. It appears the Sinclairs and MacKays are about to go to war."

They walked in silence for a bit. Then Stefan stopped and turned to her. "What did you do to me?"

Morvan blinked. "Do? I tended to your wounds."

"Nay. You touched me and...you calmed me."

She looked at the ground and gave a shake of her head. There was no use denying it. "I tend to the animals of these woods."

"Meaning?" he pressed in a soft voice.

"I heal them or help them if they're trapped."

"Like my hare earlier?"

She jerked her gaze to him, once more finding herself ensnared by his hazel gaze and thick, dark lashes. "I didn't know it was yours. There is nothing special about me. I merely take the time with the animals, and I'm calm with them. That in turn calms them."

He took a step toward her, closing the distance so their bodies were nearly touching. His gaze was probing, searching. "Call it what you will, but there is something special about you, Morvan. No one has been able to pull me back like you have. And both times, only with a simple touch."

"Pull you back from what?" she asked softly.

"You saw me. You saw the monster I become when my fury gets ahold of me."

"How often does that happen?"

"Any time I get angry."

She could feel the heat coming off him. He was intense, forceful, and dangerous. He set her on edge, and he made her ache for something she couldn't name. It was a growing feeling inside her, one that began the day before.

"What makes you angry?" she asked.

One side of his mouth lifted in a smile, but there was only desolation in his eyes when he said, "Everything."

He turned and continued on their path. Morvan fell in step behind him, wondering what turned a man like Stefan so furious all the time.

"I'll make sure you're safe," he said over his shoulder. "Then I must leave."

Morvan knew she should leave well enough alone, and yet she found herself asking, "To return to your clan?"

"Nay. I'm hunting the gypsy who ruined my life."

Morvan decided it was best to keep from asking more questions. She kept up with his fast pace, even as her ribs ached. The tea she'd drank that morning, and again at noon before the MacKays arrived at the cottage, was helping control the pain. But only just.

Not once did she ask Stefan to slow. She hoped she would be able to shake the gloomy feeling once they crossed onto Sinclair land, but it only grew with every step she took.

When dusk came, Morvan looked up to discover that Stefan had brought them back to the cliff where she'd first seen him. Thankfully, he didn't make the climb up.

"We'll stop here for the night," he said.

When he started to walk off, she stood in his path and gave him a shove back. "Sit so I can look at your wounds."

It looked like he might argue for a moment, but then he sat on a boulder and lifted a brow.

Morvan first looked at the damage he had done to his previous wounds before she examined the fresh ones. "The new ones don't look that bad, but I need more herbs for your leg and the wounds on your chest from this morning. Stay here until I get what I need."

To her surprise, she didn't have to go far to gather the herbs. As she made her way back to the cliff, she happened to see Stefan stand up. His shirt was gone and water dripped down his bare chest from the small pool of water where he had been washing.

She let her gaze wander over his finely sculpted muscles from his shoulders and arms, to his chest that narrowed to a V at his waist. She was too intent on his wounds before to notice the many scars that crisscrossed his entire torso. Despite the scars – or perhaps because of them – his body was amazing. He was a warrior in the truest sense of the word. She didn't know of another who could fight a group of men twice in one day and come out the victor both times.

She let her eyes slowly travel back up his chest, her hands wishing they could feel his warm skin, to know the shape of his muscles. When she looked into his face, Stefan was staring at her.

Morvan wasn't a maid. She'd once given her heart – and her maidenhead – to a man she'd thought loved her. Even if she were a maid, she would've recognized the desire in Stefan's eyes.

It had been so long since she'd felt such yearning stir that she feared it as much as she craved it.

Stefan tossed aside something that Morvan only belatedly realized was his ruined shirt. She walked to him, their gazes never breaking. When she reached him, she pushed him back to sit on a rock and knelt between his legs. She saw a droplet of water fall from the end of his hair to his collarbone. Without thinking, she covered the drop with her finger and spread it over his chest.

His skin was warm, his chest hair crinkling beneath her palm. Morvan's blood pounded through her as desire coiled tightly.

She went from wound to wound washing them and packing them with herbs before taking more of her shift to use as bandages. Every time she touched Stefan, it became harder and harder to keep her hands from him. He was like a magnet drawing her to him.

There were no words spoken. She felt his gaze on her face even as she kept her eyes on his magnificent body. If she looked up, she might give in to the desire that was slowly consuming her.

When she finished dressing his wounds, she set aside the herbs. After a moment, she lifted her eyes. She didn't flinch away when his hand cupped one side of her face. He pulled her to him the same time he lowered his head. Their lips brushed once, twice, seeking, searching.

A moan rumbled in Stefan's chest as his arms wound around Morvan and pulled her closer. He deepened the kiss, the passion flaring high, the desire erupting brightly.

CHAPTER FIVE

Stefan knew he should soften the kiss, but he couldn't. The longing, the desire was too great. Touching Morvan affected him in ways he couldn't describe, but kissing her set his blood afire.

Her hands roamed over his back, her touch both gentle and needy. His cock jumped when she shifted again, bringing their bodies tightly together. He ground his arousal against her and then moaned as her nails dug into his back. The woman was a temptress, a siren. And he was powerless against the yearning to have her.

Stefan bent her over his arm and kissed down her throat. He watched the way her chest heaved, the way her head lolled to the side to give him access. He heard her soft moans, saw her swollen lips still wet from his kisses.

He forgot everyone and everything except the woman in his arms. All that mattered was Morvan and the passion that raged between them.

He wouldn't be content until she was writhing beneath him, until she was so sated she couldn't move. Until he looked into her nutmeg brown eyes and saw her climax reflected there.

"Your wounds," Morvan said when her hand skimmed over one of his bandages.

Stefan took her mouth in another kiss. He didn't care about his injuries. He felt nothing but pleasure right now, and that's all he would feel.

He moved off the rock to kneel in the thick grass in front of her. Morvan's kisses were like a drug, and he never wanted it to end. A moan slipped from him. He had to feel her skin against his, to see her in all her glory. Stefan grabbed a handful of her skirts and pulled them upward.

A heartbeat later, she was helping him remove her gown. She toppled over as he finally got it off. Her laughter was the sweetest sound he had ever heard, and it brought a smile to his lips.

She looked up at him before she removed her boots. Stefan swallowed hard when he caught a glimpse of her bare thigh as she rolled down her stockings. Then all that remained was her thin shift.

Stefan held his breath, waiting for her to remove the last bit of her clothing. He had seen her naked, but he hadn't looked – much to his dismay. That's what his anger did to him.

But that rage was a world away at the moment. That's how he wanted it to stay.

He unpinned his kilt and let the material fall away. When he started to lean over her, she held up a hand.

"Wait," she said and sat up.

The way she looked at him, as if she didn't think he was real, perplexed him. There was no denying the awe in her gaze, and he didn't know what to do with it.

Out of his friends, he was the last of them that women saw or even paid attention to. He wasn't sure how to react to the way Morvan reverently touched him, smoothing her hands over his chest while always being careful around his bandages.

Everywhere she touched, his skin burned for more. From his shoulders to his chest and down his abdomen she left a trail of fire. Not once did she recoil at his many scars. Not once did the light in her gaze dim.

"Magnificent." She lifted her brown eyes to his. "That's what you are."

"I'm a warrior, meant for battle and death. There's nothing good about me."

Her eyes crinkled at the corners as she rose up on her knees and cupped her hands around his face. "You are magnificent and beautiful and glorious."

Her eyes held nothing but honesty. No one had ever looked at him the way Morvan did now. Stefan slid a hand around her waist. With just a few words, her touch, and her direct gaze, she changed something within him. It didn't make sense, but nothing had since he'd encountered her.

"Are you real?" he whispered.

"Yes."

Their lips were close, the desire burning hot. Stefan took her mouth in a frantic kiss of need and...hope. He held out a hand to break their fall as he pushed her backward.

He covered her body with his, kissing her senseless while slowly working her shift up her thighs and over her hips. He'd never been so hard for a woman in his entire life.

Stefan yanked off her shift and then looked down at Morvan. He was enthralled by her curves, taken by her alluring body. Her breasts were plump, her nipples a dusky brown. His gaze stopped for a moment on the large bruise on her side that looked as if it were already healing. Her waist narrowed before her hips flared out enticingly.

Then his gaze settled on the black curls between her legs.

"By all that's holy you're a bonny sight," Stefan murmured as he cupped one of her breasts.

Morvan sucked in a breath and her eyes slid closed. Stefan massaged the globe before tweaking her nipple. She gasped, her fingers clutching his arms. He then bent and closed his lips around the turgid peak and sucked. Her hips bucked beneath him, grinding against him. Stefan moved to her other breast and flicked his tongue over the nipple.

Morvan was drowning in pleasure. Stefan was playing her body to perfection. She was lost, adrift in a sea of desire that besieged her. But she welcomed it, sought it.

As long as she was in Stefan's arms, she was safe. She couldn't explain it, nor did she want to. It was a fact, a simple truth that she knew to the very marrow of her bones.

She moaned as his continued assault on her body stirred long-buried hopes. His hands were everywhere, learning her, discovering her.

He kissed down her stomach to her sex. She lifted her head and met his gaze. There was a confident grin pulling at his lips as he parted her thighs and leaned down to kiss her where she needed him most.

Morvan dug her fingers in the grass and arched her back as the exquisite pleasure swarmed her. The intensity of it was too much, but she couldn't pull away with the way he gripped her hips. She was powerless to do anything but endure the relentless, decadent pleasure of his tongue.

She was mindless with need, her desire coiled tightly. Her body lay open for Stefan to do with as he saw fit. The carnality of his tongue as it teased her clit, the sensuality of his fingers holding her, took her to a place she had never been before. A place she hadn't known existed.

The orgasm came out of nowhere. She jerked, a scream locked in her throat as her body shook with the force of the climax. When the last tremor finally left her, she opened her eyes to see Stefan leaning over her.

His long, dark hair hung around his face, and his hazel eyes blazed with hunger. Morvan was captivated, fascinated.

Enchanted.

He reached for her, and she eagerly went to him. Sitting up, she wrapped her arms around his neck and her legs around his waist. He held her with ease, his large hands sensuously rubbing her buttocks.

There were no words between them. They didn't need any. Everything they felt and experienced was through their eyes and touch.

It was erotic, carnal. Wanton.

Morvan felt the head of his arousal at the entrance to her sex. She held her breath as Stefan slowly lowered her until she had taken all of him. Looking into his hazel eyes, she felt as if it were just the two of them in the whole world.

Then he began to move.

Stefan didn't know what heaven was, but with Morvan in his arms, he figured it was as close as he would ever get. He couldn't stop touching or kissing her. And the way she looked at him made him want to pluck the moon from the sky for her.

He groaned at the feel of her slick, tight sheath. She was all passion and curves, and she spurred his desire with just a touch.

He wanted – needed – to hear her cry out from the pleasure again. He yearned to see the bliss light her from the inside out. Never had he seen anything so beautiful.

His thrusts grew harder as he went deeper. Morvan's lips were parted, her skin flushed. With sweat slicking their bodies, Stefan drove them toward the pinnacle of ecstasy.

Stefan unwound Morvan's legs from his waist and flipped her onto her hands and knees. He came up on his knees behind her and ran his hand from her neck down her spine to her butt.

She looked over her shoulder at him, a gleam of excitement in her brown depths. He took his cock and guided it to her entrance. Then he entered her with one thrust. Morvan groaned and pushed back against him. Stefan grabbed her hips and began to drive into her. The louder she moaned, the harder he plunged.

He leaned over her and skated his hand along her neck to turn her face to the side so he could give her a hard kiss. When he pulled back, she met his gaze and licked her lips. He very nearly spilled his seed right then.

He sank deeper into her as she rocked back against him. He could feel his own climax building quickly, but he refused to give in.

He continued to pump his hips, driving into Morvan until he felt her sheath clamp down on him. Only then did he give in to his body and allow himself to climax. As he poured his seed inside her, experiencing more pleasure in that one moment than he had in his entire life, he realized two things.

He would do anything for Morvan, and she had taken a piece of his soul.

CHAPTER SIX

Morvan lay nestled back against Stefan's chest. She couldn't remember ever feeling so happy. If she tried, she bet she could walk upon the clouds.

She took a deep breath, and it wasn't until she released it that she realized there was no pain.

"Why do you live alone?"

Stefan's question was spoken in a soft tone, but it startled her nonetheless. She shrugged. "It's how it has always been."

"Always? I find it hard to believe you've been by yourself since you were an infant."

Morvan turned to face him, tucking her arm beneath her head as she did. "I was found in the forest by an old woman named Maria. She didn't have any family of her own, so she kept me. My clan thinks I was left by the Fae."

"You never knew your parents?" he asked with a frown.

"Nay."

"Perhaps it's better that way."

Morvan guessed that he had no idea how telling his words were.

Stefan touched her cheek. "So, Maria raised you?"

"Until I was eight. We were out gathering wood after a heavy snowfall. Maria was old, and even though I could've gotten the wood myself, she insisted on coming. She slipped on the ice and fell. She never woke up."

His forehead furrowed deeply. "Surely one of your clansmen took you in after that?"

"They've always been afraid of me," she said with a smile. "It doesn't bother me."

"You've lived on your own this entire time?"

"I have." She smoothed a lock of hair back from his face. "What about you? Tell me of your family."

His gaze slid away. "There's no' much to tell. My mother died when I was ten and six."

"And your father?"

"Wouldna claim me."

Morvan covered his fist with her hand. "You obviously didn't let that stop you from becoming a warrior?"

"I was quickly becoming the monster you witnessed earlier after my mother died. The rage was steadily consuming me." His eyes returned to her. "Then I met my friends, Ronan, Daman, and

Morcant. We were all from different clans, but somehow we became like brothers. They alone helped me remember who I was."

She had the distinct feeling that something bad had happened to them. "You speak as if they're dead."

"I doona know if they live or no'. I'm going to find out right after I find the old gypsy."

"You mentioned a gypsy before. What does she have to do with it?"

He skimmed a finger down her side to her hip. "She cursed us. Ronan and Morcant disappeared first, and then she looked at me. I heard her voice in my head, and then I was in a place as dark as the deepest night where no light found its way. There was only silence and darkness."

Morvan knew about the gypsies. Maria used to tell her to stay far away from them because they only brought trouble. And death.

"How did you get out of the darkness?"

Stefan shook his head and glanced at the rocks above them. "I'm unsure. One moment I was there, and the next I was on top of the cliff."

An uneasy feeling assaulted her. "And how long were you in the darkness?"

"I estimate a few years. I couldna judge the passing of time without any light. I concentrated on my hatred of Ilinca, and it fed the beast within me, growing my fury until it consumed me. Until you touched me."

Morvan tucked the stray hairs from her braid behind her ear to keep them from tickling her face.

"What year was it when Ilinca cursed you?"

"1427."

Morvan rolled onto her back so Stefan wouldn't see her worry. Two hundred years. How could he have been locked away somewhere for two hundred years?

Her gaze snagged on the boulders high above them and the narrow, steep path she had climbed to the top of the cliff. Something had driven her there a few days ago, and she was beginning to suspect it all had to do with Stefan.

"What is it?" he asked.

"I never come onto Sinclair land. It is forbidden with the threat of war," she whispered. "Yet, I was drawn here yesterday. To the top of that cliff. I walked a maze of boulders that seemed to move on their own until I came to a wall of markings." She turned her head to look at him. "They were of Celtic design, and there was one I couldn't resist touching. The wolf."

Stefan blinked slowly. "My mother called me a wolf."

"It was after I touched the etching of the wolf that I saw you."

He inhaled deeply. "Everything I did brought me across your path. I found you last night unconscious outside your cottage and brought you inside."

No wonder she had a hole in her memories. She hadn't been awake for them. "It was you who took off my clothes."

"You were shivering," he said with a hint of a

smile.

"And this morning? Was that you I felt watching me at the loch?"

He nodded.

Morvan laced her fingers with his. "You said that the year was 1427 when the gypsy cursed you. Stefan, it's been a lot longer than a few years since that happened."

"How long?"

"The year is 1609."

His entire demeanor changed. He rolled onto his back and stared at the stars.

Morvan wasn't sure if he wanted her near or not, but she recognized that he was hurting and she wanted to offer comfort. She scooted closer and rested her face against his shoulder. The sounds of the night filled the silence as he wrapped an arm around her.

~ ~ ~

Stefan was up and dressed by the time Morvan woke the next morning. He hadn't slept at all after she told him what the year was.

Before he'd had a mission – to kill Ilinca. Regardless that the gypsy had magic, there was no way she was still alive. Stefan wasn't sure what he was going to do now. Without Ilinca, he couldn't find his friends.

They could be anywhere, in any time.

He expected to feel only anger, but there was also sadness...and despair.

"I should look at your wounds," Morvan said.

Her voice pulled him from his thoughts. He looked over to find that she had dressed. Stefan returned to the same rock as the night before and sat. He looked over her head, thinking of the future and what he was going to do while her gentle hands moved from wound to wound.

"I don't understand."

Stefan looked down. "You doona understand what, lass?"

She sat back on her haunches and lifted her gaze to him. "Your injuries are all healed."

Confused, he looked down at his thigh and saw only a scar visible. He then inspected where one of the injuries had been on his arm, and another on his chest. Each one he looked at was the same – healed.

"How?" he asked as he looked at her.

She shook her head. "I'm not sure, but it explains why my ribs no longer hurt."

"Your bruise? Is it gone?"

Morvan slowly nodded. "There is barely any discoloration."

Stefan looked up at the cliff. "You were drawn here, and I appeared here. What is this place?"

"I don't know."

"Well, we can no' stay. I know where the castle is. We should go there."

"Nay," she said and scrambled to her feet. "I'm a child of the forest."

Stefan saw the fear on her face. He assumed it was the thought of going to a new clan. He stood and grasped her shoulders. "They doona know you, Morvan. You can no' return to your clan, so you must choose whether to go to another clan, or take your chances here and tell them all you know of the MacKays."

"I don't know anything."

"I guarantee you know more than they do."

She looked down and nodded. "What will you do?"

There was really only one choice for him. "I'm going to return to the place I was cursed and start looking for Ilinca or any gypsy who can help me find my friends."

"Good," she said, but her smile was forced and tight.

Stefan didn't want to leave her, but what kind of friend would he be if he didn't look for the men he considered his brothers?

"Which way to the castle?" she asked.

Stefan pointed and walked around her. "You could have a good life with the Sinclairs."

"I'm a child of the forest. It's where I belong. I never feel…right…unless I'm in the forest."

He glanced back at her, but she wouldn't meet his gaze. For all that she had done for him, he was shattering the glow from their night together.

A few moments later, she stopped and picked some berries. She handed a handful to him and picked some for herself. Stefan was starving. He hadn't had a good meal since he got out of the darkness, but then again, he was used to missing meals when needed. He should've realized Morvan needed to eat. What an idiot she must think he was to forget such a thing. So much for him taking care of her.

It just proved that he did need to leave her in more capable hands. No matter how much she calmed the monster inside him, no matter how she'd changed his life, he would only destroy her life.

They walked for another hour until Stefan saw the castle. He stopped on the rise of the next hill and waited for Morvan to draw even with him.

"You really think they'll take me in?" she asked. "What if they think I'm a spy?"

"I came here yesterday. The people," he started and saw an old gypsy woman standing off to his right. She was staring at him, her black eyes unblinking and her gray hair pulled away from her wrinkled face.

"The people what?" Morvan asked.

Stefan quickly glanced at Morvan, but then looked back off to his right. Only, when he looked for the gypsy again, she was gone. He cleared his throat as every instinct within him urged him to find the gypsy. "The people looked happy, if no' a little anxious, but that's understandable with the threat of battle."

"What's so important out there that you won't look away?"

He faced forward and shrugged. "Nothing. Shall we go to the castle?"

"Nay." Morvan faced him and smiled. "I'll be fine. Go find your friends, Stefan."

As he looked down at her, he realized he wasn't ready to part ways yet. Before he could put his thoughts into words, Morvan rose up on her toes and kissed him.

She put her cheek against his. "Be safe, my wolf."

Then she was gone. Stefan watched her walk away. He couldn't decide whether to go after her or Ilinca, and the longer he stood there, the harder it was for him to go after Morvan.

He didn't leave until he saw her reach the gates of the castle. What had he heard the people call it? Ravensclyde. It was a grand name for an impressive castle.

Stefan released a breath when Morvan was admitted into the bailey. Now that she was safe, he could focus on Ilinca. Stefan turned his back on the castle and walked to where he'd seen the gypsy.

~ ~ ~

Morvan touched her chest. There was an ache there that felt as if someone had yanked out her heart. Stefan had come into her life as quickly as he left it. She didn't regret a single minute she'd shared with him, but that didn't help the emptiness within her now.

She wasn't just empty without Stefan, she was lost without the forest. Morvan closed her eyes and pictured the tall pines, the thick birch, the sturdy oaks. She imagined ferns on the ground and the constant chirping of birds. The woods would help to heal her. If she could get back to them.

How, when she was homeless? She had nothing but the clothes on her back. The Sinclairs had welcomed her into Ravensclyde, but it wasn't her home.

"Morvan?"

Morvan opened her eyes to find herself meeting a gray gaze. The woman that addressed her was frowning, concern showing in her gray depths. Her red hair was pulled back in a loose bun. That's when Morvan remembered entering the bailey and introducing herself to two women.

"She doesn't look well at all," said a second voice.

Morvan shifted her gaze to the left and saw another woman with long brown hair and sky blue eyes. "I'm fine."

The redhead snorted. "You're as pale as death. Come inside so we can feed you," she said and took one of Morvan's arms.

The brunette took the other, nodding as she did. "Food, aye. That's what she needs."

Morvan let them lead her into the castle, but she wasn't seeing any of the people or the gray stones. All she could see was hazel eyes, long dark hair, and a breathtaking body.

"Eat," said the redhead as she shoved a trencher of food at Morvan.

When had they sat? Morvan glanced around nervously.

"It's not poisoned," said the brunette who reached over, pulled off a piece of meat and ate it.

"I'm Leana."

"And I'm Meg. You told the guardsmen that you came to Ravensclyde from the MacKays."

Morvan nodded as she bit into the bread. Her stomach growled loudly as she chewed and swallowed. "I came to warn you that Donald MacKay is planning to attack."

"Again?" Leana asked worried, her gaze on Meg.

Meg's lips thinned. "He's already tried that once, and we defeated him."

Morvan hadn't known that.

"I saw Morvan's arrival, but not another attack," Leana said.

Morvan's gaze jerked to Leana. "You saw me?"

"I have...dreams," Leana explained. "I had a vision of you coming here to Ravensclyde two days ago."

Two days ago? That's when she was on Sinclair land and went to the cliffs. Stefan. Why did it feel as if all of this revolved around Stefan?

"Do you know why I'm here?" she asked Leana.

The brunette shook her head. "I see only glimpses. Did you just come to tell us of Donald?"

"Aye." They didn't need to know about Stefan. He was her secret, a stranger she'd conjured from the darkness and tamed – for a time anyway.

"Why?" asked a deep voice behind her.

Morvan turned around and saw two men standing with their arms crossed over their chests. They were imposing men, but after seeing Stefan fight, nothing could impress her anymore.

"Why?" the man with the pale green eyes and brown hair asked again.

Leana walked to the second man who had sandy blond hair and topaz eyes. "I told you about my vision. This is her."

The first man's gaze didn't waver from Morvan. She set aside the bread and said. "There was a stranger that came onto MacKay land. A small group of warriors came upon him and tried to kill him. He was...ferocious in his fighting and killed all but a few who ran back to Donald. I found the stranger after the fight and bound his wounds."

The man lifted a dark brow. "Then?"

"I left the stranger to go about his way. It isn't in my nature to leave an animal in pain unattended."

"He wasna an animal," stated the blond.

Morvan shrugged. "If you'd seen him fight, you would think otherwise."

The two men exchanged a glance. Then the dark-haired one asked, "I'm guessing Donald discovered you helped this stranger?"

"He did." Morvan swallowed, remembering how Stefan had so effortlessly saved her life. "Donald is...unforgiving. He threatened to burn me alive."

Meg touched her hand. "What happened to bring you to us?"

"The stranger," Morvan said. "He saved me."

The dark-headed man dropped his arms. "Where is this stranger? I'd like to talk to him."

"He's gone." Morvan felt the weight of the words, and they hurt far more than she'd expected – far worse than leaving the forest.

CHAPTER SEVEN

Stefan got as far as the stream before he came to a halt, unable to go any further. No matter how hard he tried, he couldn't take another step.

He couldn't stop thinking of Morvan, of how her nutmeg eyes held no anger or censor – just acceptance. She hadn't looked back when she'd walked to the castle. He knew because he had watched her every step of the way.

Without moving from the tree line, Stefan stared at the quick moving stream. It was the place where Morvan had changed his life. One touch had altered his entire course.

He looked to the sky to see night descending. Stefan turned on his heel and started back toward the castle.

~ ~ ~

Morvan rubbed her eyes and sat up from the comfort of the bed. She glanced out the narrow window of her room to see that the sun was high in the sky. It wasn't like her to sleep past dawn.

She rose and dressed, then brushed out her hair. She had embarrassed herself the night before, by falling asleep as Meg and Leana were talking to her.

Was it a dream, or had Meg introduced her husband as Ronan? It had to have been her thoughts of Stefan and her exhaustion mixing with her arrival at Ravensclyde. The more she thought about it, the more she couldn't clearly remember the name of Meg's or Leana's husband.

It was beyond rude to fall asleep on her hosts. But after the two women kindly brought her upstairs, Morvan had found a bath. It was all she could do to stay awake as she washed the day off her, but she managed it before climbing into bed.

She'd missed dinner, of that she was certain. And it was clearly a new day. How long had she slept?

Morvan tied off a strip of leather at the end of her braid and walked to the door of her chamber. She opened it and stepped into the corridor. It was the sounds of the hall that drew her in the direction of the stairs.

Those at Ravensclyde wanted Stefan's name, but she wouldn't give it. He had been detained long enough. He needed to find his friends. Morvan longed for the forest, to feel the bark of the trees against her palm and hear the wind moving through the leaves.

But the Sinclairs needed to know how dangerous Donald was.

Once she descended and stepped into the great hall, Morvan didn't know what to do. Neither Meg nor Leana was in sight. Morvan followed a delicious aroma to the kitchen and snagged some bread before she walked to the bailey. She stood against the castle wall and simply watched everyone.

It was odd for her to be in the company of so many and not have them look at her with scorn. Perhaps Stefan had been right and this was a new start for her. No one at Ravensclyde knew about her, and they didn't need to.

Morvan lifted her face to the sky and breathed in the air. She missed the forest, but she didn't expect to live her life in the castle. Until she was able to answer the questions Meg's and Leana's husband had of her, she would remain.

After that...she wasn't sure what she would do. Perhaps she would see if there was a vacant cottage in the forest. If not, maybe she would build herself something.

As she turned to go back inside the castle and look for Meg, there was a shout from near the gatehouse. Morvan looked and saw a horse rearing, its hooves pawing the air in a bid to get free.

The horse pulled free from the two men holding him and started running. Morvan looked behind her and saw a group of children frozen in fear as they watched the oncoming steed.

Morvan stepped in front of the white horse and began to hum even as she heard a shout from the castle steps. She ignored whoever was telling her to move away and hummed louder. The horse slid to a halt and reared again.

She shifted to keep from having a hoof hit her when the horse landed. Morvan put her hand on the steed's shoulder, rubbing his white hair. He jerked his head up and down twice, shaking his long dark gray mane before he blew out a breath and remained still.

His big black eyes closed when she ran her hand along his back. She saw the scars on the horse's mouth, legs, and back. He was abused. No wonder he was so wild.

"It's all right," she whispered as she rested her head on his neck. "I won't let anyone hurt you now."

"You either have a death wish or a gift," said a deep voice behind her. "Which is it, lass?"

Morvan glanced over her shoulder to see Meg's husband. So much for the people of Ravensclyde not knowing about her ability. "I'm sorry for falling asleep on you last night. I apologize, but I can't remember if we were introduced. I'm Morvan."

"I'm Ronan, and the halfwit with his mouth open in surprise behind me is Morcant."

Morcant grunted. "I'm no' a halfwit. She amazed me is all. Hell, Ronan, she shocked the entire bailey."

Morvan continued to rub the horse, the action

calming her as much as the frightened animal. Morcant and Ronan. What were the odds of finding two men with the same names as the ones Stefan searched for? Was Daman around somewhere, as well?

She met Ronan's pale green gaze as he came to stand beside her and held out his hand for the horse to sniff. Ronan waited for the horse to accept him before he gently rubbed the steed's forehead. "You doona have to fear us here, Morvan. As Leana told you last night, she has visions. Whatever gift you have is welcome."

"Where is Daman?"

There was a flash of astonishment in Ronan's gaze before his face lost all emotion. "You've seen Daman?"

"Nay, but the fact you know the name means you also know the fourth one." She wasn't going to say Stefan's name on the off chance that it was all a coincidence.

Ronan looked at Morcant over his shoulder. A moment later, Morcant stood with them.

"Stefan," Morcant said. "The fourth's name is Stefan."

Morvan's knees buckled. She only managed to stay on her feet thanks to her hold on the horse's mane.

Ronan's brow furrowed as he leaned closer. "It was Stefan who helped you, was it no', Morvan?"

"Aye," she whispered. "He's the stranger I spoke of yesterday."

Morcant rested his hand on the hilt of his

sword. "We need to go after him, Ronan."

Ronan nodded, but didn't take his gaze from Morvan. "Where did he go? Is he returning here?"

"He was on his way back to the place where it all began," she said.

Morcant let out a string of curses. "We can still catch him."

"Be careful," Morvan cautioned. "He can be a bit untamed."

Ronan's lips compressed. "We know firsthand."

She watched the two men stride off, hoping they were able to find Stefan quickly. Morvan walked the horse to the stables herself and fed him after putting him in his stall.

By the time she returned to the castle, she was exhausted. She was quickly surrounded by Meg and Leana who guided her to the solar.

"Is it true?" Leana asked her. "Is Stefan out there?"

Morvan nodded. "It is. The past few days have felt like someone aligned the stars to bring us together."

"How do you mean?" Meg asked.

Morvan told them the story of how she'd been brought to the cliffs by some unknown force, and how she and Stefan came to meet. She left out their night together, ending the tale with Stefan leaving her at the castle.

"He was here," Leana said with a shake of her head. "He was right here. If only he had come in with you."

Morvan picked at a sweetmeat. She had

consumed four during her story. "He was so anxious to find his friends. All he wanted to do was get back to the place where it all began to see what he could find."

Meg leaned back in her chair, regarding her. "How much did Stefan tell you?"

"All that he knew. Was he right? Were they cursed?"

Leana sighed loudly. "They certainly were."

It took all Morvan could do to keep her eyes open as the two shared their stories of how Ronan and Morcant came to be at Ravensclyde.

"Is it fate that all three were brought to this clan?" Morvan asked.

Meg smiled. "It's magic."

Magic. Morvan wasn't sure if that was the correct word, but then again, she didn't know what to call whatever had compelled her to the cliffs to touch the etching of the wolf.

"Are you feeling well, Morvan?" Leana asked worriedly.

Morvan rubbed her hand along her forehead. "For some reason I can't shake the exhaustion."

"It's everything you've been through." Meg rose and helped Morvan to stand. "We'll let you rest in your chamber."

Leana smiled. "And we'll be sure to let you know as soon as Stefan arrives."

~ ~ ~

Stefan spent the entire day trying to make it

across the stream. The farthest he got was half way before he got a bad feeling. As soon as his feet were back on Sinclair land, the feeling dimmed, but didn't go away.

He bedded for the night at the cliffs, but sleep eluded him. All he could see when he closed his eyes was Morvan as they'd made love beneath the stars in that exact spot.

Stefan was on his way back to the castle before the sun peaked over the mountains. He waited for a glance of Morvan, because he knew she couldn't stay within the castle walls for long. She was a child of the forest, after all.

As the sun continued its ascent, there was no sign of her. Stefan decided to try a different route to leave. Surely this time he would make it back to the glen where he and his friends were cursed.

If he couldn't have Morvan, he could at least avenge his friends.

CHAPTER EIGHT

For four days, Stefan tried to leave. He tried going different directions each time, but every dawn he found himself back at the castle hoping for a glimpse of Morvan.

He'd stayed at the castle longer than he should have, especially since there seemed to be someone following him. Stefan briefly contemplated waiting for whoever it was, but he didn't want to fight. He just wanted to see Morvan.

As the dawn of the fifth day came, Stefan walked from the trees across the open plain to stop a cart that had just come from the castle.

"Good morn," he called to the elder man, putting a smile on his face though he felt like anything but smiling.

The man nodded in return. "Good morn."

"There've been rumors around that someone from the MacKay clan has come to the castle. Is it true?"

The old man looked back at the castle for a moment. "Aye. It's a woman who came. It must be bad at the MacKay clan for their people to begin coming to Ravensclyde."

Stefan patted the horse pulling the cart. "What does the laird say?"

"The laird isna here yet, lad. He and his men will be here soon enough, I wager. If clan MacKay wants a war, they're going to get one."

Stefan had seen enough of death. He wanted to be as far from the battle as he could. Now he wondered if it had been a good idea to leave Morvan at Ravensclyde. "What have they done with the woman?"

"She's in the castle," the old man said and snapped the reins.

Stefan let him drive off. He walked back to the forest and circled the castle, his gaze on the battlements. The longer he went without seeing Morvan, the more worried he became.

Were they keeping her prisoner? Were they hurting her?

It was time he found out.

~ ~ ~

"She's not waking," Meg said as she wiped a wet cloth across Morvan's forehead.

Leana stood beside the bed, her face pinched

with frustration. "I've tried all the herbs I know. Nothing is working."

"We have to do something. If we don't, Morvan is going to die."

Leana looked at all of the herbs sitting around the chamber. "I don't know what else to do, Meg. She's pale as death already. And I don't know what's wrong with her."

"We've gotten some water down her. That's something at least, right?"

Leana licked her lips. "It's not going to be enough."

~ ~ ~

Stefan was on his second round of the castle when he realized whoever had been following him had found him once more. If he took the time to confront them, it would be longer before he could get to Morvan.

He didn't understand the sudden urgency he had to reach her, but he wasn't going to waste another moment. It was essential that he get to Morvan immediately.

With his mind so focused on Morvan, he didn't realize how close his pursuer had gotten until the point of a sword pressed into the back of his neck.

"Slowly turn around."

Fury ripped through him. Who was this bastard that was going to keep him from Morvan. For five days, there hadn't been a seed of anger in him.

Until now.

Stefan spun around, ducking as he did. He came up and slammed his fist into the chest of his attacker, sending him flying backwards.

A second man stepped forward. Stefan threw his elbow back into the second assailant's throat. Then he fully faced his opponent and reared back his hand to punch him when the first man jumped on Stefan's back and held his arms so Stefan couldn't punch.

"Easy!" the man shouted.

Stefan, however, was long past the point of controlling his anger. The monster was back. He bared his teeth and lunged for the second man who was coughing. Then he thought of Morvan. He didn't want to be a monster anymore. He wanted to be a man worthy of her, one who could control all his emotions – especially his anger.

And just like that, his anger diminished.

Not that he was going to let the two men attacking him win. Stefan got an arm loose and elbowed the man on his back.

"Stefan, please!"

It wasn't his name that got his attention, but the voice. There was something recognizable about it.

"Look at Ronan," the man said. "He willna be able to talk for a few days after that hit you landed in his throat."

Stefan shook his head. Ronan? He blinked several times.

"That's it, brother. Look at Ronan. Hear my voice. We didna let you succumb to your monster before. We willna let you now either."

"I'm in control," Stefan said calmly as he looked into the pale green eyes of Ronan. Despite his coughing, Ronan smiled. It *was* Ronan. It wasn't a dream, but the man himself. And the man on Stefan's back was none other than Morcant.

"Control, aye?" Morcant asked as he slid off Stefan's back. He came around to stand in front of Stefan, a bright smile on his face. "You *are* in control. We didna think we'd ever catch up with you. By the saints, it's good to see you again."

He allowed himself a few seconds as Morcant embraced him, pounding him on the back. Stefan then faced Ronan, helped him stand and motioned to his throat. "I'm sorry."

Ronan waved away his words and roughly pulled Stefan close so he could embrace him.

Steven couldn't believe he had his friends, his brothers back. He looked around, waiting for Daman.

"He's no' here," Morcant said. "Ronan was first, and I came a few months ago. Now it's you. All of us were drawn to Ravensclyde, so we're hoping Daman will be, as well."

Stefan faced the castle. "Morvan. I need to get to her."

Ronan slapped him on the arm and walked around him as he said in a hoarse voice, "Come."

"Nay. I need to be there now. Something is wrong," Stefan said glancing at the castle again.

Neither man questioned him. They raced to the castle. As soon as the guards saw Ronan and Morcant, they opened the gates to let them through.

Stefan followed his friends into the castle and up the stairs to a chamber. He threw open the door and felt as if someone had kicked him in the stomach when he saw Morvan lying so still upon the bed.

There were two women with her, but Stefan paid them no heed. He walked to the bed and tenderly lifted Morvan in his arms. "I shouldna have left you," he whispered.

"We're glad you're here," she said the brunette. "I'm Leana, and the one with Ronan is Meg."

"Thank you for looking after Morvan." Stefan turned to his friends. "She's a child of the forest. I need to get her there quickly."

"The forest is near," Meg said while standing next to Ronan.

Stefan noticed Leana stood with Morcant. Two of his friends had found women. He glanced down at Morvan. Somehow, he wasn't surprised. He had found much more than a beautiful woman. He'd found peace, and...love.

"I need to take her to the cliffs. The last time we were there, both of our injuries were healed. It's also the place where she pulled me from the darkness."

Morcant took his woman's hand and nodded to Stefan. "Lead the way. We'll do whatever you need."

Stefan walked out the castle doors and down the steps. There was a commotion near the gatehouse, and a horse came running out of the stables.

"No' again," Morcant said.

But Stefan wasn't concerned. "Morvan helped him."

"How did you know?" Leana asked.

Stefan waited for the horse to reach them. "Because the animals she helps never forget her."

He walked to the horse and smiled when the steed lowered himself into a bow so Stefan could climb upon his back with Morvan still in his arms.

Stefan grabbed the horse's mane in one hand. "We'll go to the cliffs."

He raced beneath the gatehouse and heard the sound of horses behind him. Stefan didn't need to look back to know it was Ronan and Morcant. Although he didn't realize until the horses drew even with him that Meg and Leana were on their own mounts.

The six of them entered the forest. Stefan saw the color begin to come back into Morvan's face, but it wasn't enough. She needed whatever magic was at the cliffs. For whatever reason, the cliffs were magical. They hadn't just compelled Morvan there, they had gotten her to release him from the darkness.

It felt as if an eternity had passed before he saw the cliffs. As soon as they reached them, he swung a leg over the horse's neck and slid to the ground. Stefan walked to where he and Morvan had made love, but nothing happened. He looked up at the cliffs.

"You'll never make it up there holding her,"

Ronan said.

Stefan looked at his friends. "I have to try."

"Then we'll help," Morcant replied.

Stefan was about to tell them he would do it himself, but then he remembered why he considered them his family. "All right."

Ronan and Morcant didn't even try to dissuade their women from accompanying them. Together, all four of them helped him get Morvan to the top.

He was sweating, his muscles fatigued by the time they reached the crest. Despite the fact he hadn't remained at the top long the first time, he recalled the tall boulders and the narrow passages.

Stefan led the way until he eventually found the wall Morvan had spoken of. He stood looking at all the carvings in the rock as the others fanned out around him.

"I doona know what this place is, but it led Morvan to me, and it has led me back to her." Stefan kissed her forehead and turned to lean against the wall.

Then he slowly lowered himself until he was sitting with Morvan in his arms. "With one touch she calmed the monster within me. I was in a fit of bloodlust and was after her. I was going to kill her because I couldn't control my anger. I grabbed her, and that's when the haze of fury cleared. I can't lose her."

Morcant squatted beside Stefan. "You said she's a child of the forest. You've brought her back. She'll be all right."

Stefan looked into Morcant's eyes before he

turned to Ronan. "If she doesna live, you'll have to kill me. You both need to understand that. The grief mixed with my anger will be too much. I willna be able to be stopped."

Ronan put his hand on Stefan's shoulder. "We've no' let you down before. We willna this time either."

Stefan pulled Morvan closer. "You didna just give me peace, Morvan. You showed me gentleness and kindness. But your greatest gift was your love. Come back to me. I willna ever leave you again."

Hours faded with the daylight. With each passing hour where Morvan didn't wake, Stefan felt his anger try to stir. He refused to give in to it. He no longer cared about Ilinca and getting his revenge. All that mattered was Morvan and the new life he wanted with her.

Ronan and Morcant had found him, but more importantly, Stefan had found Morvan. For the first time in his life, he prayed. Long and hard.

The stars were bright overhead when Morvan finally shifted her head. Stefan's eyes snapped open. He held his breath, ignoring the four others sitting around the fire.

"Morvan," he whispered.

Her eyes slowly opened to meet his. "Stefan."

He couldn't contain his joy as he ran a hand down her face. "How do you feel?"

"Better. You came back?"

"Aye."

She nodded. "You figured out that Ronan and Morcant were here."

"I came back for you. I tried repeatedly to leave, but I could never get verra far. My mind was filled with you. It took me long enough, but I realized that I couldna leave you. You touched my soul, Morvan. You gave me a gift I thought I'd never have."

She was very still as she whispered, "What?"

"Love. I love you more than life itself. I know I'll have to earn your love, but I'm prepared to do whatever it takes."

She put her finger over his lips to stop him from talking. "You've already done all that you could. I saw you," she said, placing her hand over his heart. "I felt you. There is nothing else for you to do, Stefan Kennedy, because I already love you."

He couldn't believe fate had finally smiled upon him, but he wasn't going to question it. Stefan brought his head down to her lips and kissed her.

Morvan's arms wrapped around his neck and he deepened the kiss. Dimly, he heard the sound of four sets of footsteps leaving. Then he didn't care as the desire took them.

EPILOGUE

Morvan climbed down the cliffs with Stefan. They had passed the hours of the night with lovemaking, talking, and more lovemaking. She was pleasantly sore, and the look in Stefan's hazel eyes whenever his gaze met hers made her stomach flutter.

He had said she saved him, but in truth, she thought it was the other way around. She inwardly chuckled as she recalled him telling her that they had the rest of their lives to debate it.

As Stefan lifted her off the last boulder to the ground, Morvan faced Ronan and Meg and Morcant and Leana who had remained at the base of the cliff. They were all smiling.

Ronan cleared his throat. "At this point with Morcant, I asked him and Leana to come to the castle to help me fight the MacKays. I doona think that offer will be accepted by you."

"Nay," Stefan said and looked at Morvan as he tightened his grip on her hand. "Our place is in the forest."

"We'll help in the coming battle," Morvan said.

Stefan raised a brow. "You want me to fight?"

"They need you."

Morcant rocked back on his heels. "Are you no' afraid of his monster returning?"

Morvan cupped his face. "That's what I'm for."

"Then I guess we'd better get busy building you and Stefan a cottage," Meg said.

Ronan glanced up at the cliff. "As close to the castle as we can, right?"

They all laughed at the comment. Morvan looked up at Stefan as he pulled her against him. Fate had been leading her toward Stefan. For all those years she'd thought she would spend her life alone, it was all worth it to finally have the love of a man like Stefan.

"What of Ilinca?" she whispered.

Stefan shrugged. "I'd rather focus on you, and them," he said with a jerk of his chin to Morcant, Leana, Meg, and Ronan.

"And Daman."

Stefan nodded slowly. "And Daman. I'll find him."

Morvan didn't have any doubts. If all three of them had found their way to Ravensclyde, the odds were good that Daman would, as well. She couldn't wait until all four of them were back together again.

Stefan was happy, but he wouldn't be complete until Daman was found.

The air stirred around her, and Morvan knew that the old gypsy wasn't finished with the four men yet.

Look for the next Rogues of Scotland story –
THE SEDUCED – Coming February 9, 2015!

Daman scratched his jaw and ignored the
thunder and lightning that had been on display over
the next mountain for the past half hour. The knot
in his gut about the gypsy camp only intensified the
longer he was there.

Something bad was going to happen. He knew
it just as sure as he knew the storm coming in
would last for an entire day. The sooner Ronan,
Stefan, and Morcant were finished with the women
the better.

Daman wouldn't make the mistake of returning
with his friends again. And he would do his best to
prevent them from coming back as well. Perhaps a
talk with the gypsies was in order. They were on his
clan's land.

Three hours had already passed already. It was
time for he and his friends to leave. Daman rose
and walked between the wagons to get their
attention. Then he paused.

In the middle of the camp was a large fire and
many of the gypsies sitting around it. Two were
playing the violin in a hauntingly eerie song that
somehow kept in time with the thunder. Among
the gypsies was Stefan who stared into the fire as if
searching for something. An old woman sat off by
herself, her gaze on the wagon Ronan had entered
hours ago.

Unease prickled Daman's skin.

He wanted to leave, but he wasn't going to go without his friends. Some unknown, unnamable emotion was coursing through him. Every instinct told him they needed to leave. Immediately.

Daman rose and walked to the edge of the camp. He looked at the ground, then up at the wagon where Ronan and Ana were. He could shout out Ronan's name, but his friend wouldn't answer even if he heard him.

Daman's gaze slid to Stefan. With Morcant busy, he could get Stefan's attention, but Stefan was talking to three male gypsies. Besides, Daman didn't need help. All he had to do was cross the boundary and get his friends.

He looked up at the sky and stared at the thousands of stars. The moon was only a sliver in the night, leaving the land cloaked in darkness. Daman ran a hand through his hair and returned to the tree. As long as it took, he'd wait for his friends. Then he'd get them away.

No sooner had that thought crossed his mind than the night was shattered an anguished scream. It was filled with despair and fury dragged from the depths of Hell itself.

Daman's blood ran cold, because he knew his apprehension was becoming fact. He looked from Stefan to Ronan, who was exiting the wagon. Ronan was shirtless and standing outside Ana's wagon with a hand on the hilt of his sword. Ronan looked at an old woman who stared at something in the grass.

Daman reached the edge of the camp when Morcant exited a wagon still fastening his kilt. Something bad was coming for them.

Daman searched the ground for where Ronan and the old woman were looking. The bright pink and blue skirts of Ana, Ronan's lover was visible from the dim light of the fire. As was the dagger sticking out of Ana's stomach.

The odds of any of them getting out of the gypsy camp without a fight wasn't in their favor. By the looks exchanged between the gypsies, they were prepared to die to avenge Ana – regardless that Ronan didn't kill her.

Daman looked to Morcant and Stefan and saw the slight nod of Stefan's head. Morcant slowly began to pull his sword from his scabbard as Ronan shook his head in denial.

"Ronan," Stefan said urgently, palming the hilt of his sword, and waited.

There was a moment of silence, as if the world held its breath.

Then the old woman let loose a shriek and pointed her gnarled finger at Ronan. Ronan's eyes widened in confusion and anger.

Daman heard a gypsy near him whisper a name – Ilinca – as he stared at the old woman. Ilinca's face was contorted with grief and rage.

Words, hurried and unfamiliar, fell from Ilinca's lips. The language was Romany, and by the way Ilinca's dark eyes narrowed with contempt, it was a curse she put on Ronan.

Daman waited for Ronan to grab his sword and

the battle to begin. When nothing happened, Daman looked harder and realized Ronan being held against his will. His pale green eyes were wide with confusion.

Daman opened his mouth to shout to the others, but Stefan drew his sword the same time Morcant rushed Ilinca. The old gypsy shifted her gaze to Morcant, and he halted awkwardly, her words freezing him in place.

Once Morcant was taken care of, her gaze returned to Ronan and continued speaking in the strange language.

"Stefan!" Daman shouted.

But it was too late. Stefan's fury had been let loose, and the monster was free. Stefan released a battle cry and leapt over the fire toward Ilinca. Stefan hadn't gotten two steps before the old gypsy pinned him with a look that jerked him to a halt instantly.

Then the old woman's gaze turned to Daman. He sighed and thought of his friends. There was one rule between the four of them – they lived or died together. Daman stepped over the boundary, a cold tremor rushed down his spine at Ilinca's triumphant smile.

He was immediately surrounded by men. Undeterred, Daman left his sword in the scabbard and used his dirk and his hands to slice, stab, punch, and kick anyone stupid enough to get close.

Five men fell – two dead. He put another three on the ground before he found his limbs immobile. No matter how hard he tried to move his body, he couldn't.

The men parted, and Ilinca walked to him. Daman looked around, but Ronan, Morcant, and Stefan were gone – vanished as if they never were.

He glared down at the old woman. How he wanted to tell her how he was going to kill every last gypsy he came across as punishment for what she did to his friends, but the words wouldn't come. Ilinca controlled every bit of him.

"Why didn't you enter the camp?" Ilinca asked him.

His eyes narrowed as he realized she had allowed him the ability to speak. She wanted answers, but he wasn't going to give them to her. His lip curved in a sneer.

"So, you don't want to answer. You don't like to ask for help, do you? Your friends have been cursed, but you already know that." Ilinca drew in a breath and looked him over closely. "Why did you have to come into camp? You were wise enough to keep out earlier."

Daman saw her hands shaking. Her eyes were bright with unshed tears. She was upset at Ana's death, but he was desperate to find his friends. Even if it meant talking to her. "Where are the others?"

"Some place they can't hurt anyone or themselves."

"Ronan didna kill Ana."

Ilinca lifted her chin. "He might not have stuck the blade in her, but he's still responsible. Just as Morcant is responsible for bedding an innocent and ruining the chance to align our people."

Daman tried to move his arms, but she still held him in place. "And Stefan?"

"You know the answer to that better than anyone else here. His rage."

"What are you going to do with me?"

The old woman stepped closer and the gypsies closed in around him. "I had a vision a week ago of this very night, though I didn't see my granddaughter's death. I knew each of you four have something important to do."

"Do? I'm no' important."

"I can only repeat what I know." Her shoulders drooped. "My magic will ensure each of you reach your destination. What you do there is up to you. You can be freed. Or you can spend eternity in your prison."

Daman got that bad feeling again as Ilinca placed her hand on his forehead. He wanted to jerk away, but she still held him frozen. His eyes grew heavy, and the more he fought to keep them open, the more tired he became.

"Don't fight it, Daman," Ilinca's voice whispered in his head.

It was his nature to fight. He fought against it, but it was too much. The world went black like the snap of someone's fingers.

Ilinca sighed as she dropped her hands and took a step back from Daman. Then she nodded and the men carried him to her wagon and brought him inside. Grief rose up in her like a tidal wave. She would tend to Daman later. Right now she needed to bury her granddaughter was buried.

Once that was done she had a destination to reach.

"Grandmother?"

Ilinca held out her arms for Ana's younger sister. When Amalia wrapped her arms around her, Ilinca held her tight. "It's almost over, my sweet."

"You didn't say Ana would die."

"I didn't know." Ilinca didn't stop the tears from falling. "Ana impetuous and kind, but she wasn't strong like you are."

Amalia looked up at her. "Where did you send those men?"

"Far away."

"And the fourth? Why didn't you send him?"

Ilinca glanced at her wagon. "Because he's the key to all of it."

Thank you for reading **The Tempted**. I hope you enjoyed it! If you liked this book – or any of my other releases – please consider rating the book at the online retailer of your choice. Your ratings and reviews help other readers find new favorites, and of course there is no better or more appreciated support for an author than word of mouth recommendations from happy readers. Thanks again for your interest in my books!

Donna Grant

www.DonnaGrant.com

ABOUT THE AUTHOR

New York Times and *USA Today* bestselling author Donna Grant has been praised for her "totally addictive" and "unique and sensual" stories. She's written more than thirty novels spanning multiple genres of romance including the bestselling Dark King stories, *Dark Craving, Night's Awakening,* and *Dawn's Desire.* Her acclaimed series, Dark Warriors, feature a thrilling combination of Druids, primeval gods, and immortal Highlanders who are dark, dangerous, and irresistible. She lives with her husband, two children, a dog, and four cats in Colorado.

Connect online at:

www.DonnaGrant.com

www.facebook.com/AuthorDonnaGrant

www.twitter.com/donna_grant

www.goodreads.com/donna_grant/

Never miss a new book
From Donna Grant!

Sign up for Donna's email newsletter at
www.DonnaGrant.com

**Be the first to get notified of new releases and
be eligible for special subscribers-only exclusive
content and giveaways. Sign up today!**